TALES FROM THE BERLIN WALL

Recollections of Frequent Crossings

Marianna S. Katona

Illustrations by Tamara Fodor

Anotam, Berlin

The cover photo: "Kingsheads" - was taken by Heinz J. Kusdas in 1985 at Waldemarstrasse in West Berlin. It shows a stretch of the Wall with murals by Kiddy Citny.

Katona, Marianna S:
TALES FROM THE BERLIN WALL: Recollections of Frequent Crossings. Illustrations by Tamara Fodor. – Berlin: Anotam, 2003
ISBN 3-8334-0439-6

First Published 1997 by MINERVA PRESS London
Republished 2003 by Anotam Berlin

ISBN 3-8334-0439-6
Copyright: © 1997, 2003 by Marianna S. Katona
              All Rights Reserved
Layout: Jörg Sperling *SperrowSoft* IT und Medien, Berlin
              info@sperrowsoft.net
Production: Books on Demand GmbH, Norderstedt
Printed in Germany

TALES FROM THE
BERLIN WALL
Recollections of Frequent Crossings

For Sári and Gabi, in memoriam Burk

Acknowledgments

First and foremost, I thank David Antal, language scholar and knowledgeable historian, for helping me put these stories into readable form. Not being a native speaker but still wanting to communicate in English, I needed a competent editor. Luckily, David took up the task of tightening and straightening my sentences. Moreover, he advised me on several aspects of the Allied presence and policies in Berlin.

I am also indebted to Catarina Kennedy-Bannier, who, while translating the manuscript into German, weeded out many inaccuracies in the passages relating to events in East Berlin and in the descriptions of conditions in the former German Democratic Republic. I value her spirited involvement in the project.

The book has greatly profited from communication with Hagen Koch, founder of the Berlin Wall Archive, who filled several gaps in my memory about the regulations in the 1960s and 1970s and provided me with valuable information about the operation of the crossing points. Pictures and maps from his archive make this book more authentic. Other photographs were obtained from The Berlin Photo Archive (*Landesbildstelle Berlin*) with their kind permission.

I am grateful to relatives and friends who joined in recalling the events that we experienced together so long ago.

One always needs a motivational push to start a project. On a tour with foreign visitors, I once related my most memorable experiences of Checkpoint Charlie, mentioning that I intended to write them down some time. Lars Rydén from Uppsala asked the ultimate question: "When? What are you waiting for?" So I started writing.

Encouragement along the way was also necessary and welcome. I appreciate all the suggestions and corrections from those who examined earlier versions of the manuscript. Special mention is due to my faithful young readers – Soscha Antal and my daughters Sári and Gabi – who waited for the completion of each new chapter with curiosity. Their interest and inquisitiveness convinced me that it was worth the effort to continue.

While thankfully acknowledging the input of these supporters, I emphasize that I alone am responsible for any errors that may remain in the text.

About the Author

Marianna S. Katona was born in Budapest, Hungary. After the Hungarian revolution in 1956, she emigrated to the United States, where she joined her uncle in Ann Arbor, Michigan. She studied mathematics and chemistry at the University of Michigan and married a German economist. The couple lived alternately in Germany and in the United States before settling in West Berlin in 1977. There, Ms. Katona earned a doctoral degree in crystallography from the Free University of Berlin. While raising two children, she has held research positions in computing and crystallography on either side of the Atlantic and is currently working at the Institute for Crystallography of the Free University of Berlin.

Contents

Introduction

"Imagine what happened to me at the border!" was a regular conversation topic at West Berlin gatherings until November 1989. It was almost a contest to find out who had a more gruesome inconvenience while crossing over to or coming back from East Berlin, where one went to visit relatives, attend the theater, hear an opera, see a museum, or take visitors on a sightseeing tour. But there were also determined natives who stated with conviction: "I haven't been in East Berlin since the Wall was built, and I do not intend to subject myself to these harassments."

For over two decades I have been planning to write down the experiences I had crossing the border. Until 1990 the list steadily grew, but now the memories are starting to fade and gaining historical perspective. Just as in a biography, both the beginning and the end are known after the protagonist dies; now that the Wall is gone, the number of my experiences cannot increase anymore, unless I invent some tales, which I do not intend to do.

How did I, a foreigner, come to accumulate all this 'data'? I certainly didn't plan a journey to Berlin with journalistic or sociological ambitions. It was fate, I think. In 1960, at a Christmas party in the Ann Arbor home of my uncle, who was a professor at the University of Michigan, I met a tall, handsome German student who was spending a year in America on a Fulbright fellowship. He had escaped from East Germany in 1953, as I had escaped from Hungary in 1956. We had several topics of common interest, and after many walks and talks together, a few days before my graduation from college in June 1961, he asked me to marry him. I could only answer with a 'maybe', but I promised to visit him in Germany after I had received my Master's degree and my American citizenship in the spring of the following year. He planned to return to Cologne in September to complete his doctoral dissertation.

My boyfriend studied economics, but his father, one brother, and several uncles and cousins were physicians. The brother, Peter, lived in East Berlin and worked in a hospital as an ear, nose, and throat specialist. His father had a private practice of the same specialty in

West Berlin. In August 1961, Peter was commuting to his father's practice, who was on vacation in West Germany. Overnight from Saturday to Sunday, August 13th, a barbed wire barrier was erected that halted civilian traffic and cut families off from each other. Next day Peter had to send a telegram to his father: "Come back urgently, I cannot get to your practice anymore." Peter's next visit to West Berlin took place in 1965, when he received special permission to attend his father's funeral.

When I first arrived in Berlin in the summer of 1962, Peter's parents had not seen their son for a year. The barbed wire had already been replaced with the first-generation wall, which consisted of cement blocks topped by barbed wire. The East Germans called it the 'Antifascist Protecting Wall'; the Westerners called it 'The Wall of Shame' (*Schandmauer*). Daring people tried to overcome this obstacle, with varying success, by climbing it, or sliding over on a cable, or tunneling under it. Sad memorials still stand along the one time course of the Wall to remind the world of those who lost their lives in the process. To the single-strand wall another strand called the hinterland wall was added further back on eastern territory. This pair of walls stood until the end, but the original cement blocks were replaced by prefabricated, horizontal cement slabs topped by a cement tube. This ensemble, identified later as the second-generation wall, gave way by and by to the third and final generation of the wall's design: vertical slabs of reinforced concrete over ten feet (3.4 meters) high. Because of its smooth surface, this version was ideal for graffiti. On some stretches on the outskirts of Berlin, the Wall was composed of a similarly high wire-mesh fence. Between the parallel strands was the 'death strip', a minefield[1] of fine 'desert sand' interrupted only by a narrow tarred road in the middle for the guards to move around. At special places, mostly where disrupted streets ended at the Wall, the death strip was fortified with anti-tank barricades to make sure that powerful armored vehicles couldn't break through the twin concrete strands to continue on the

---

[1] The East German authorities never refuted the assertion that this area was indeed mined. It is now known, however, that the circumference of West Berlin was not mined, just the border between East and West Germany, and even that much only until 1984. The myth about a minefield around West Berlin has survived anyway and is still occasionally repeated during sightseeing tours.

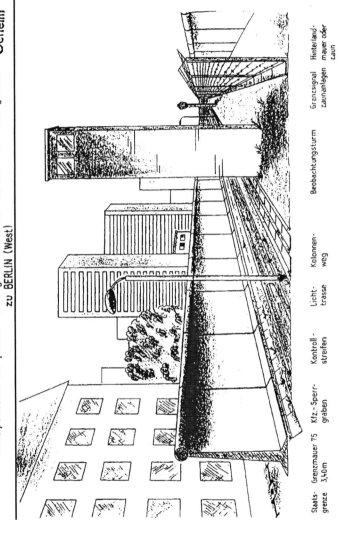

Plan of the Wall from East German archives marked 'Secret' (Geheim)

street that still existed on the other side. The entire death strip was. illuminated with bright street lamps that, from a distance, seemed like a well-lit boulevard or the place of some important sporting event. Guards with loaded guns sat in tall watchtowers overseeing this desolate territory. Twenty-eight miles (45 km) of wall divided the city in the middle, and an additional seventy-five miles (120 km) surrounded the rest of West Berlin, separating it from East Germany.

The desert sand didn't have to be carted in from the seashore because the ground in and around Berlin consists of fine sand. Each construction site in the city where the thin top soil has been removed looks like a huge sandbox.

It took a lot of effort for the German Democratic Republic (GDR) to maintain the desert conditions, because the climate is nothing like that of the Sahara. There is plenty of rain, and seeds from the forests and meadows nearby are easily carried by the winds. When the Wall was torn down in 1990, city officials were worried that the death strip was so saturated with herbicides that it would remain a desert for a long time. Fortunately, a chemical analysis didn't turn up the feared high concentrations, and the death strip gradually turned green by itself. First some wild flowers and grass appeared; later shrubs and small trees replaced the erstwhile 'Berlin Sahara Strip'.

Maiden Voyage

The ink had hardly dried on my American citizenship papers in the spring of 1962 when I applied for the ultimate dream and treasure of East Europeans, a passport to see the world. Through a New York agency I booked passage on a freighter, the least expensive ocean crossing available at the time. The ship was called the *Carsten Russ,* and it belonged to a Hamburg shipping company. The trip from Baltimore, Maryland, to Hamburg, Germany, was to take fourteen days non-stop.

I took a taxi from the train station of Baltimore to the designated pier and looked startled when the taxi stopped at the edge of a big black cloud.

"Where is the ship?" I asked timidly. The taxi driver pointed into the darkest center of the cloud.

"Right there, loading coal." In my imagination a ship was supposed to be white against the vast blue of the ocean, but this one was a hardly visible gray outline. Still, I bravely entered the cloud, walked onto the ship, and opened a door that seemed to be the entrance to the passenger area.

"Close the door, otherwise the coal dust comes in," greeted me.

The inside was clean and my cabin comfortable. Looking into the mirror later that evening, I discovered that I looked like a chimney sweep.

It surprised me no end that the ship carried coal from West Virginia to Germany; my school education and a college course in economic geography had informed me that Germany was a major coal mining nation. But actually the latter course also helped me to understand that cheap mining and a long sea route could beat the more expensive German mining and shorter, but still expensive, rail transport. In any case, the fact was that some electrical power plant near Hamburg burned coal dust from West Virginia in 1962, and I was one of seven passengers on a freighter carrying such coal. The crossing was pleasant, and I used it to practice my limited, bookish knowledge of German with the crew members. After disembarking in Hamburg, I went to visit Brussels, London, Zurich, Geneva, Vienna, and Cologne. At last, the time came to be introduced to my 'maybe' future parents-in-law in Berlin.

My boyfriend, his brother Ulrich, the brother's fiancée and I drove from Cologne to Berlin in a tan Volkswagen bug. In West Berlin I was put up in a hotel instead of at the home of one of the relatives, because we were not engaged yet. The rather dismal hotel pension was on the second floor of an apartment house on Kottbusser Damm, near my future parents-in-law's apartment on Oranienstrasse in the Kreuzberg district.

A strong explosion rocked my bed and woke me in the middle of the night. First, I tried to quiet myself, thinking, 'Don't worry, turn over and sleep.' I then performed some quick accounting in which it occurred to me that I was in the Cold War's capital of crisis and less than a mile from the Wall. It made my mind go around fretting about the start of the Third World War. According to some, a recently discovered escape tunnel had been blown up that night to make it unusable. Just a few weeks before, in June 1962, four people had escaped, but many more were arrested at the first use of a 40-meter-long tunnel that surfaced in a West Berlin building site on Kochstrasse. I was also told that Western political activists periodically blasted holes in the Wall to protest its presence. Whichever was the real reason for that night's explosion, I never found out for sure.

Next day the time came to visit my boyfriend's relatives in East Berlin. My enthusiasm was limited because less than six years had passed since I had escaped from Hungary, and I had not been back behind the Iron Curtain yet. My fear was stronger than my curiosity.

To complicate matters, my boyfriend asked me to take his brother's car over with me at Checkpoint Charlie, the crossing point for foreigners, because there the line-up of cars was shorter than at Prinzenstrasse, the checkpoint for West Germans. Because I had so far driven only large American cars with automatic transmissions, he asked his mother to teach me the use of the gearshift and then lined up with the pedestrian transit crowd. I duly took over the wheel and practiced driving up and down Kochstrasse, grinding the gears in my novice's attempts to master the art. With my future mother-in-law getting more and more nervous, I drove her home and decided to ruin the car alone. I soon took the plunge into the line-up at Friedrichstrasse leading up to Checkpoint Charlie.

In front of the first boom barrier, I presented my brand new US passport. It was my protecting umbrella, a camouflage of the defector from the Eastern bloc. The guard looked at my passport, then glanced at me, then again at the passport, at me again, and asked, "Are you related to the Hungarian Olympic swimmer Katona?"

This struck me like lightning. I had already been discovered as a Hungarian refugee. Not yet inside the Eastern control area, I could turn back, if I only knew how. Where was the reverse gear anyway? "No," I stammered, "I have never heard of him." At that moment the barrier was raised. The next car was so close behind me that the only possibility was a forward gear, so I entered the GDR with shaking knees. Thinking back on this 'confrontation', I was surely too fretful. The guard had probably been a swimmer himself and may have merely wanted to chat about my namesake rather than arrest me on the spot. Actually, it was very unusual and probably even forbidden to converse with the public. For years the style was either interrogation or giving orders, like, "Take off your sunglasses," or, "Open the trunk." Maybe he was a beginner at his job, as I was a beginner at crossing back and forth between West and East.

Another 'almost conversation' followed an hour later with another guard when I finally emerged from the passport check barrack. Still too nervous to think straight, I climbed into the car, started it, put it into reverse, and stepped on the gas pedal. The car rocked slightly, but then the engine stalled. On the second attempt I gave more gas but got no further. On the third attempt I tried to let the clutch out more slowly, but the engine stalled each time. A guard came over and asked: "Can you drive?" By this time I wasn't sure but still replied "Of course!" and repeated the futile maneuver. Then he looked into the car and pointed out that my handbrake was on. I thanked him, released the handbrake and shot out backwards from the parking space. Forward driving had to be very slow and careful. To assure reduced speed in later years, after some armored vehicles broke through the border checkpoint (from East to West, naturally), a slalom course was set up.

Without a map, it was hard to find Heinrich-Heine-Strasse, the continuation of Prinzenstrasse in the East, where my boyfriend was waiting for me. He said that I should keep close to the Wall and just find the next place where traffic was coming through. There was no street along the Wall that I could follow, so I adopted the strategy of first driving straight ahead, turning right, then right again to see if the street dead-ended into the Wall. If it did, I then turned back and did the same at the next opportunity. Still, I got lost and found out the hard way that the streets of the two checkpoints were not parallel. The whole situation seemed unreal. 'Where am I and what am I doing here?' I asked myself. It felt as if I were part of a spy movie. My zigzag search took me along ruins, deserted areas, and big empty squares with large construction sites. Practically no pedestrians were to be seen, but fortunately hardly any cars either until I reached the correct street. It took quite a while to get there, but my boyfriend's crossing also took more than an hour, so he did not have to wait for me very long.

I complained that the driving practice had been too much for his mother and the real driving too much for me and that he should therefore have taken the car himself. He insisted: "But I knew that you could do it! You got here right on time, and the car is fine. What's the problem?" Maybe there was no problem, but I felt as if I had just scaled Mt. Everest.

Marriage Contract and Name Change

Two months after my first visit to Berlin, the Cuban missile crisis broke out. It started practically on the first anniversary of the confrontation between American and Soviet tanks at Checkpoint Charlie. Each of these crises ended on October 28th, one in 1961, the other in 1962. The tank confrontation erupted when East German frontier police turned back employees of the US Mission because they refused to produce identity papers upon demand. This action by the East German officials violated the Four-Power military agreement of unhindered allied passage between the sectors. General Lucius D. Clay, the American Commandant in Berlin, ordered US tanks to the checkpoint. The Soviets lined up tanks of their own on the other side, and the world held its breath.

The Cuban missile crisis was a similar stand-off, but it took place on the high seas with naval vessels. President Kennedy placed a naval 'quarantine' on Cuba, preventing the continued delivery of offensive long-range missiles to the island by Soviet ships. While a serious military mobilization was under way in the United States, the Soviets backed down. Their ships turned back, and the missiles already in place in Cuba were dismantled. Although the immediate danger had passed, it still seemed at the time that the next crisis with an uncertain outcome could be just around the corner.

Against this political backdrop in October 1962, my answer was expected to the question of whether I would get married to my German boyfriend and move to Germany. During my introductory visit to Berlin we had a very good time, and the would-be relatives were all friendly to me, but I fretted all the time. The large detonation during the first night and the many tanks and jeeps that rattled on the streets all over the city awakened childhood traumas in me.

As a very young child during the last two years of World War II, I did not know who was shooting whom or why, and my earliest childhood memories from that period include frightening noises. I understood that people around me had no influence over this clamor, and the danger of dying was formulated in my mind clearly: 'Just as lively chickens end up boiled or fried, the same may happen to us if a bomb or burning airplane comes our way.' The grown-ups had been very effective in communicating fear and danger to us children.

My dolls and toys all perished in the bombing of Budapest, fortunately without my presence. In the countryside, where I spent 1944, we had no fortified shelters, so my brother and I spent the air raids under a heavy oak table on a porch. From this hiding place we once watched a burning airplane streaking down the horizon, luckily not onto our table. The war stopped when the Soviet Army marched into our village in October 1944, but the noises of war still continued. Men and equipment moved through daily towards Budapest, and we also had soldiers staying with us overnight once in a while. After one of these 'visits', during which jeeps and trucks filled our small yard, I found a very interesting toy. For several months my only plaything had been an empty shoe polish box, so the exploration of this new object occupied me fully. My brother, later an engineer, also became very interested, but we didn't initiate the grown-ups into our dissection of the 'object'. Our secret became public when the thing exploded out of my hand and, after a much larger detonation a second later, filled the room with smoke. The 'toy' turned out to have been the detonator for a hand grenade. I escaped without a scratch, but an old visitor was badly wounded on her foot.

These and other war experiences returned in many variations as nightmares for several years. Slowly, the unpleasant dreams stopped and gave way to the live 'nightmares' of the Stalinist years. Shooting started again in 1956, when the Soviet Union brutally suppressed the Hungarian uprising that demanded free speech and free elections. This time we spent a week in the sturdy air raid shelter of a large apartment house. We lived on the Pest side of the Danube, well within range of the powerful Soviet guns placed on a hill of the Buda side in the twin city of Budapest. Five direct hits shook our building, broke all the windows, demolished four apartments, and filled the cellar with dust and smoke. It also killed two people, who for reasons of their own had not joined us in the basement. When the fighting was over, Soviet tanks started round-the-clock intimidating promenades on the banks of the Danube, the boulevards, and the bridges. The noise was nerve-racking, and the future seemed hopeless. My parents, brother and I escaped from Hungary to Austria by walking across the border at night. The mind-grinding tanks and the illegal border crossing generated another five years of nightmares. Hardly yet recovered, I was in Berlin in the midst of a large military arsenal with masses of soldiers ready for action.

I told my friend that I couldn't live in Berlin and that if he planned to settle there then I wasn't the right partner for him. He assured me that he had no chance of a job in Berlin and that if we were to get married we would never move there. This promise was one part of our verbal marriage contract, the other one being my promise to him never to bring a dog or a cat into our household. We kept the part about the pets, and in 1962 our move to Berlin was still fifteen years away. We celebrated our engagement on Oranienstrasse in West Berlin in February 1963 and were married in Ann Arbor, Michigan, in August of the same year. After the wedding, we settled in Cologne and soon planned a visit to my new parents-in-law.

In those days it wasn't possible for a married woman to keep her maiden name, so I soon sent my passport together with my marriage certificate to the American Embassy in Bonn for a name change. Several days after the expected return date, I called the embassy and asked when the passport might be sent back. They told me that they had sent it out a long time ago. The delay was inexplicable because the mail was quite fast and efficient in those years. So the next day I went downstairs to confront the mailman with my inquiry. He remembered that a few days before he couldn't deliver an envelope from the American Embassy because the apartment number was missing and the name was not one of those listed on the mailboxes. In spite of the name change, the officials had addressed the envelope with my maiden name!

This first calamity was soon followed by a second. On our way to Berlin, we parked our car at the East German transit control point Helmstedt/Marienborn[1] and entered the processing barrack. A guard

---

[1] Throughout this text some border-crossing places are referred to with two names, their Eastern designation and their Western one. Which of the two names comes first depends on the side from which the described crossing is taking place.

checked the passports and sent people into long lines sorted alphabetically. A glance at my passport landed me in the line at the K window, while my husband was sent to the S queue. After an hour's wait we each advanced to our designated windows. A most unfriendly officer asked me what the asterisk and extra sentence "See page seven for changes" meant near my name. I showed that it referred to page seven, where my newly acquired married name had been entered. He remarked angrily: "Then your name starts with an S and not with a K; you are at the wrong window!" I told him that I was there because another officer, with whom I didn't want to argue, had sent me there, but that if I had to get processed at the S window, then he should please help me get to the window directly because I had already stood in line for an hour. No mercy, no extras. It took another hour of standing around until I advanced to the S window to get my transit visa from Marienborn to West Berlin and back again by car.

The rest of my adventures with the name change in my first US passport are not worth mentioning, but the many subsequent crossings of the German-German border may fill quite a few pages.

"You Can't Get There from Here!"

In the first years of the Wall, the rules were either not clearly spelled out or not easily available. We and many others stumbled from one blunder to the other, spending untold hours waiting in vain. One of these mistakes occurred at the transit crossing point Dreilinden/ Drewitz in 1963.

Jay S., a friend of ours from the University of Michigan, spent the 1963-64 academic year in Cologne working with my husband. During the winter recess, he traveled around Germany by train and joined us in Berlin, spending Christmas with us and my parents-in-law. Since Jay was heading back to Cologne after the holidays, just like my husband and me, it was logical that he should ride with us in our car.

On the return trip we drove to the transit booth, parked the car, and went in. This time we all lined up at the letter S and in due course advanced to the window where our passports were taken away for processing. After half an hour my husband and I had the right stamps to proceed, but not Jay. The controllers had noticed that his round-trip visa (to and from West Germany) was issued for travel by train, not by car. They explained that he needed a new visa. Then they informed us that only Germans could obtain transit visas at Drewitz, so Jay, as an American, had to go back to East Berlin to get one. This was, of course, not a generally known fact, and every traveler involved had to find it out the hard way.

Had we met the W. family before this incident, they could have warned us how this transit checkpoint operated, but only much later, during a lively exchange of hard-luck border stories, did we compare notes. Their learning experience dated from the summer of the same year. They had moved to Berlin from Austria in early 1963. Their belongings, carefully itemized for the controllers, had transited with a moving van while the family flew to West Berlin. There they had bought a Volkswagen and at the end of the school year had packed into it their four children, ranging in age from one to six years, and all the necessary luggage for four weeks in the mountains. They had headed for the same expressway exit, Dreilinden/Drewitz, that everybody used driving from West Berlin to western and southern Germany. Although the W.s had expected the border procedure to be tedious, they had never dreamt that six difficult hours lay between leaving home and crossing city limits.

The Austrians had lined up in the processing barrack with the conviction that they would get a transit visa at the head of the appropriate line. No. They were told to go to East Berlin, where a special office of the foreign ministry of the GDR would issue the visa, generously, on the same day. This meant first crossing into East Berlin by lining up at Checkpoint Charlie for a day visa, paying a visa fee, exchanging some money, and going through customs by unpacking all bags and suitcases. On a hot summer day, with four squirmy children and a heap of luggage in the car and a ten-hour drive still ahead of them, this seemed to be too much.

Checkpoint Charlie alone is a forty-minute drive from Drewitz even if the traffic is moderate. Luckily, they had some friends living in Lichterfelde, a southwestern area of the city, not too far from the expressway. They were able to 'park' all four children with these friends, so only the grown-ups proceeded to Checkpoint Charlie. Envisioning how the controllers would dig into their carefully packed bags and ask endless questions, such as why they were carrying so many baby diapers for a day-visit to East Berlin, Mr. and Mrs. W. decided to park the car in West Berlin and go on foot to the checkpoint. The crossing procedure went 'normally'. Afterwards they took a bus to the appropriate office building near the boulevard *Unter den Linden*, where they lined up again to obtain the necessary papers. The next line-up occurred for the return crossing at Checkpoint Charlie, a time-consuming endeavor at the height of the tourist season. They found their car with all its kiddy clothes still in place, drove back to Lichterfelde, packed up the children, thanked the baby sitters for sparing them from a nervous breakdown, and drove to Dreilinden/Drewitz on their second attempt to leave Berlin. They inched their way to the control booth in a long vacation queue, parked again, stood in a processing line for the fifth time on that day, and finally received the small stamp that allowed them to head for their beloved mountains.

Compared to the W.s' experience, ours was a mild case. Jay had no reason to go back to East Berlin to get a visa enabling him to transit the GDR by car, for his chance of using the highway had just been ruined by the same authorities. After all, they had just sent my husband and me on our way west to Cologne and him on his way east for the visa. Since we had already been processed, we could neither wait for him, nor drive him back to the city even if we had wanted to. Worse yet, he had to hitchhike back, because in those years there was no bus service to and from the transit point to the Wannsee subway station in West Berlin. Once Jay was finally back in the city, he went to the train station and bought a ticket to Cologne with money that he would have gladly saved by accepting our ride.

My husband and I, saddened by the loss of our travel companion, drove on in our ancient gray 'standard' Volkswagen bug, a vehicle in which we had an easy time observing the 100 km (62.5 mph) speed limit on the East German expressway because it could hardly move faster than that. The car was a hand-me-down from my parents-in-law and was affectionately known as Daddy, after its Berlin license plate letters, 'B-DD'. (The numbers that followed them have long since been forgotten.) The Federal Republic had already introduced obligatory periodic inspections for all vehicles. In Cologne, however, Daddy could still be driven despite its questionable condition because of its Berlin license plate, but its days were numbered.

The trip back to Cologne turned out to be the last journey for our indestructible VW. This car had no brake lights and no indicator lights. Intentions to turn were anachronistically indicated by arms that swung out from slots located behind the doors. A new regulation in 1963 required that these old-timers get rewired so that their tail lights indicated braking and turning. Complying with this law and bringing the car up to the technical standard needed to pass the inevitable inspection would have cost more than the old VW was worth. We drove it as it was, until the Cologne police fined us and ordered Daddy off the road.

Our transit through the GDR ended at Marienborn/Helmstedt, and we felt relieved when the last barrier was raised to release us to the West. The subsequent controls of the Federal Republic at Helmstedt were considered mere formalities. This time it was a mistake to think so. They, too, became a time-consuming, troublesome experience for us. My West German residence permit (*Aufenthaltserlaubnis*) had expired a while before, and I had not been in a hurry to get a new one. So I received a long lecture in which words like "getting deported or fined" came up. My husband tried to dispel the serious, reproachful atmosphere with some small talk and friendly conversation. He mentioned all the red tape I had to go through as a newly married new resident in Germany and promised that he would personally see to it that I complete this additional bureaucratic procedure. Then we told of our recent border trouble with our would-be passenger from Michigan. The mood softened, and I was released without a fine or a deportation notice, but the time delay was enormous. The rest of the way we had to drive in the dark, taking turns at the wheel and pulling over for intermittent naps. It was a long and unpleasant day, but we arrived a few lessons richer.

"The Baby Should Cross at Checkpoint Charlie!"

Our first child was born in Cambridge, Massachusetts, where we spent two semesters on a postdoctoral fellowship that my husband had received from a German foundation. The baby was named Charlotte after her German grandmother and Hungarian great-grandmother. Both families were especially keen on deciding whether the child carried the features of their side or of the 'more exotic' other side. Charlotte was six months old when we returned to Germany.

My mother-in-law, who had visited us in Cologne, reported in Berlin that her namesake granddaughter had delicate features and small bones 'not like one of us' but that she was still very special in a positive way. My brother-in-law in East Berlin wanted to see this exotic little creature, especially because he stated that he took esthetic pleasure in slender and small women and fine-featured children.

Back in 1965, the first visit of baby Charlotte to her uncle in East Berlin was carefully planned. Since I was preparing for some exams, my husband, the proud father, volunteered to show off his baby to his brother alone. He also wanted to demonstrate that he could take care of a small child by himself, a rather unusual feat in a traditional family in those days. Father and daughter started out in a Volkswagen bug and got to the Prinzenstrasse checkpoint.

Since we had just recently arrived from America, the baby only had a US passport, whereas my husband showed his West German papers. The stone-faced border guard said that since the child was a foreigner it had to cross at the foreigner's checkpoint, meaning Checkpoint Charlie. My husband politely thanked the man for the information and indicated that he and the baby would drive there to cross the border. "No," said the guard. "You are a West German; you cannot cross at the foreigner's checkpoint."

The baby has to cross alone at Checkpoint Charlie!

"But the baby cannot go alone," complained my husband.

"That's your problem," was the icy reply.

"Where can I cross together with my child?"

"Nowhere!"

My husband returned to Lichterfelde, where we were staying, a half-hour drive from Prinzenstrasse, and begged me to hurry up, get ready, and not forget my passport and driver's license. I suggested that he leave the baby at home with me and go alone, but he was sure that his brother wanted to see the child and insisted that we should not give in to the inhumane family-splitting practices of the GDR. So as a political act of defiance, I left my books and climbed into the car.

I dropped my husband off at Prinzenstrasse and drove with the baby to Checkpoint Charlie. In those days one had to park the car at the crossing point, go into the processing barrack and wait and wait and wait. It didn't matter if there were many or few people, the wait was never less than thirty minutes. The baby was heavy to hold for a long time, and I don't remember that there were chairs to sit on, because we were waiting in various lines.

The drive from Checkpoint Charlie to Heinrich-Heine-Strasse was again an exercise in criss-crossing the ruins of East Berlin and getting lost among them until I found my husband just emerging from his checkpoint. Finally, after a two-hour delay, father and baby were together on the other side.

"Put Two Drops in Each Nostril!"

In the early sixties, the controls at the Berlin checkpoints were strict and the waiting tedious. There were some rules stating what one was allowed to carry over as a present and what was forbidden, but the gray zone was considerable. As West Berliners, my parents-in-law were not allowed to visit their son Peter in East Berlin, so they used my husband and me as 'carriers'.

My mother-in-law reasoned that I, with my innocent looks and American passport, might be allowed to take along more unusual presents than my husband. So I was loaded down with 'gray zone' merchandise. My father-in-law received free medical samples from pharmaceutical companies, and he generously forwarded some of them – alas – through me as messenger. I never hid anything because body searches of suspicious or nervous people were general practice. I openly presented the chocolate, the oranges, and a small bottle of nose drops. The customs inspector pointed at the carton containing the bottle and asked sternly:

"What is in here?"

"Nose drops for my relatives," I said.

"You are not allowed to take it over!" thundered the inspector.

I offered to give up the offending merchandise:

"Then I give it to you as a present. When you have a cold, put two drops in each nostril." I was trying to be friendly and not sarcastic. This put our negotiation on different terms. He was allowed to confiscate anything that I carried, but what might have happened to him if he had accepted a present from an American woman? He waved his hand that I should quickly get lost, nose drops and all, and turned his attention to the next victim.

On another occasion I was the unhappy carrier of five meters of white electrical cord. In the GDR the uniform color for outside

Toy or machine?

housepaint was gray and for inside, white, but for electrical cords, there was a choice between black and brown. Because my brother-in-law had a white ceiling, he asked for some decadent Western white cord for a low-hanging lamp.

"What is this for?" asked the inspector.

"To hang a lamp in my brother-in-law's living room."

"You are not allowed to take it!"

"Then I give it to you as a present."

I got away with this approach once again.

Christmas presents from grandma to her grandsons also went through my hands. I remember standing in line with a nervously beating heart, clutching a cavernous bag with a large toy bulldozer. A few places before me a young man, possibly from Italy, started to unpack his goodies for inspection.

"What is this?" asked the inspector for the hundredth time this hour, pointing to a rectangular object.

"This is a laughing machine."

The customs officer looked puzzled and before he could think of the next question for the interrogation, the young man turned on the machine. A strong, hearty laughing sound filled the drab room. Everybody was stunned. The border personnel in these early years were always very stern; as a consequence, the transiting public was intimidated and equally stern. But at the sound of this big bru-ha-ha laugh, a slight snicker went through the spectators. The officer looked offended. Instead of laughing along, he thought he was being laughed at. He commanded:

"Turn it off and put it away!"

My main concern was the bulldozer: would the laughing machine improve or hurt my chances of getting it through? It turned out that toys were allowed but that mechanical devices were not. There ensued a long discussion over whether the bulldozer was a toy or a machine. The customs inspector tried out some of the moving parts with interest and was visibly impressed. He would have played longer, but some of his colleagues and the next in line were watching, so he accepted the 'toy version' and let me pass.

Crossing by Train: Stops and Ghost Stations

The Friedrichstrasse subway station was the largest, busiest, and most centrally located crossing point between the two Berlins. However, its location with respect to the East and West sides of the city confused many visitors. On the map it clearly lay deep inside the Eastern sector, but as far as the administration of this site went, it was a border station. Because my first experiences of the Friedrichstrasse station date from the 'walled-in' years, the place still gives me the impression of unfathomable complexity, a feeling that established itself during my years of crossing there.

Early this century the city developed not just one, but two rapid transit systems: the S-Bahn (*Stadtbahn*), meaning city railway, and the U-Bahn (*Untergrundbahn*), meaning subway. As the names indicate, the U-Bahn operates underground, and the S-Bahn runs above ground, often on elevated tracks. But both systems do have their exceptions, that is, elevated U-Bahn stretches and underground S-Bahn lines. After the Wall divided the city, both transport systems were split into an eastern and a western part, resulting in four different operations.

To confuse matters further, the western S-Bahn line was still owned by the *Reichsbahn,* the eastern railway company, until 1984. Thus until then, East Germany was one of the largest property owners in West Berlin. Of course, the S-Bahn of the East was segregated from the S-Bahn of the West, but it was possible to change from one to the other at the Friedrichstrasse station after going through tedious control procedures.

By contrast, the East and West U-Bahns were owned by their respective city transport authorities. To the total confusion of tourists, the tickets for the S-Bahn and U-Bahn companies were different, and a day ticket for all lines of the BVG, the (West) Berlin Transport

Authority, did not cover all public transportation in West Berlin, for the BVG did not run the S-Bahn. Most tourists had no idea what they were getting into when entering this labyrinth, and I witnessed some great surprises when visitors discovered at the ticket checking booth of the S-Bahn that their 'all-inclusive' tickets excluded most of the direct lines to their desired destinations. To emphasize East German ownership and to irritate West Berliners, the S-Bahn carriages ran through West Berlin festively sporting flags of the GDR and the Soviet Union on Eastern-bloc holidays.

Historically, the two transport systems had been set up to complement each other, but after the Wall went up the western administration encouraged the population to boycott the S-Bahn. Bus lines were set up along the routes to make the boycott possible. The East-German state perennially lost money on its operation of the S-Bahn and finally shut down some of the lines after Western S-Bahn employees staged a strike for higher wages in 1980. Stations started to disintegrate, and weeds took over the tracks. In 1984 West Berlin bought the western S-Bahn system and started to restore the stations one by one. The lines gradually reopened under management of the BVG, and the superfluous bus routes were discontinued.

Without passing through one of the border checkpoints, one could only reach the Friedrichstrasse station from West Berlin by train. Passengers were already tuned into the cold war atmosphere as the train traveled through 'ghost stations', at which the train did not stop. Lying deserted between the Wall and Friedrichstrasse, these once heavily frequented locations were patrolled day and night by reliable eastern border guards, mostly to prevent East Germans from escaping through the train tunnels. The outside markings of these stations had been removed, and most East Berliners didn't even know they existed.

In 1990 the ghost station *Unter den Linden* on the southern Wannsee line was renovated and opened. It had exits on Pariser Square, to the left and right of the Brandenburg Gate, so I asked a taxi driver in the center of East Berlin to drive me there. This young man in his twenties energetically declared that he knew his city well and that there was no train line near the Brandenburg Gate, so there could be no station, old or new, in the area. I didn't want to lecture him that I had observed this most depressing-looking station below ground for longer than his lifetime and had only recently discovered exactly where it was located above ground. The young man clearly had grown up oblivious to the existence of this subway line and station, and in his eyes a foreigner didn't have the right to know the public transportation better than he, so we agreed that he should just drive me to the Brandenburg Gate. From there I would walk over to the West if there was indeed no station at the assumed spot.

It is hard to imagine how the western city transportation would have functioned between 1961 and 1989 if its trains had been denied access to the Friedrichstrasse subway station. Several lines stopped at this hub and continued on their way, connecting northern and southern boroughs. The subway's nonstop passage through the ghost stations produced a certain express-train character, and commuters could even ignore the fact that they traversed East Berlin twice daily. Passengers could also freely change trains at Friedrichstrasse within the western system. A freaky specialty of the D-platform at the lowest S-Bahn level was the *Intershop* run by East German authorities. Here one could buy duty-free liquor, coffee, and cigarettes with West German currency. To catch the carriers of large amounts of duty-free merchandise, considered illegal in West Berlin, local police made some spot-checks on trains when they emerged on western territory. One way to avoid carrying around alcohol in bottles is to have the stuff already inside you. Alcoholics from West Berlin populated the platform of the *Intershop,* making the place even more depressing. Violent scenes that often erupted between them were broken up by the patrolling GDR border personnel.

Whereas the lowest levels in this complex terminal belonged to the Western S-Bahns and U-Bahns, the upper level, once a 'through' station of several lines, was divided into two end stations. The line coming from Wannsee on a northeast route was forced to end there, just as several eastern lines could not proceed westward. The big vaulted glass structure of the station was divided by a non-transparent wall so that the eastern passengers could forget that there was a world they were not allowed to enter, or even to peek into, on the other side. Only the eastern terminal was directly connected to the street, allowing pedestrians to come and go without controls.

The platforms of an international railway terminal were on the western side. Strict inspections took place at the entrance, and the

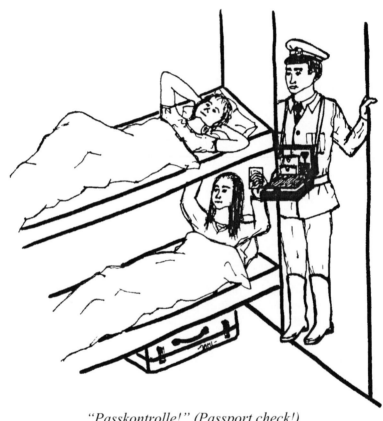

"Passkontrolle!" (Passport check!)

passengers in the trains were also checked because Friedrichstrasse was a 'border station'. A traveler on the Paris-Warsaw route had to show his passport in Germany six times: first to western authorities when entering West Germany, and usually again when leaving the country at Helmstedt. The eastern authorities looked at the passports and filled out a visa form as the train entered East Germany at Marienborn, just after Helmstedt. Another control was conducted when leaving the GDR at Griebnitzsee and entering West Berlin at Wannsee. One had hardly put away the papers by the time the train was again on eastern territory, namely at Friedrichstrasse, East Berlin, for another passport check. For good measure, a final check occurred at Frankfurt/Oder just before leaving the GDR and entering Poland. Those who traveled this stretch overnight cannot forget the violent knocking on the doors of the sleeping compartments announcing the *Passkontrolle,* a noise that could raise the dead and almost killed the living through fright.

"Here You Don't Get Served, You Get Processed!"

Between the upper and lower train stations at Friedrichstrasse, there was the control point, but where? Stairways, corridors, and barricaded passages formed a maze with armed guards standing all around. The crossing str store: "Where does one get served here?"

The guard corrected sharply: "Here you don't get served [*bedient*], here you get processed [*abgefertigt*]!" – an unforgettable sentence that we repeated many times in similar situations. I got a lesson another time when, likewise lost in the flow of the crowd, I asked, "Where is the way to East Berlin?"

To this, the schoolmarmish answer came: "To the capital city of the GDR, straight ahead and then to the right!" We had to orient ourselves not only in a physical maze, but also in the right expressions. In the West the correct names were: Berlin (West) and East Berlin, on the other side it was Westberlin and Berlin, capital of the GDR.

The style of the processing changed several times between 1961 and 1990. In the sixties one had to wait in designated areas with processing numbers after handing in one's personal papers. The numbers were called up through ill-functioning loudspeakers to return the documents with the desired visas. If somebody had a hearing or a language problem, then it could happen that his or her papers landed again at the bottom of the heap. I always suffered anxiety when separated from my passport in this hostile environment. As a one time refugee, I never got rid of the feeling that my identity as a free person was intact only with a US passport in my pocket.

In the sixties, Berliners of either side could cross only for special occasions and only with special permits, so the bulk of the transiters were West Germans and foreign tourists. Many popular British and American spy novels dealt with the communist-capitalist conflict as carried out in the divided city; tourists flocked to the scene of these thrillers to thrill themselves by seeing the 'enemy' in action. They entered the processing catacombs with a mix of curiosity and fear. Sometimes I had the impression that they went there as they would to the zoo, where one is particularly pleased when the lion isn't resting during the visit but letting out a few roars and eating some bloody meat. On one crowded, but otherwise uneventful, morning all heads turned with excitement when a young Englishman was asked to empty his pockets. Keys, loose change, a billfold, and some papers came to light. Among the papers was an unopened letter. The controller asked: "What is in this letter?"

"How should I know?" answered the would-be visitor in relatively good German. "It only arrived this morning, and I haven't had the time to open it."

"Open the letter!" was the next command. The man obeyed and the guard took a searching look at it. Most probably he couldn't understand a word of English, but after inspecting the letter he was satisfied that all potential secrets could have been uncovered had he understood the contents.

The written word was the most dangerous commodity that visitors could carry with them into the GDR. The customs officer asked at each checkpoint: "Do you have books or magazines with you?" My husband always answered that he hadn't, even when he accidentally left the daily newspaper on the back seat of his car. The case was so obvious that he wasn't penalized for it, but when he said "no" at Friedrichstrasse and his newly published book was found in his canvas bag, between coffee and oranges, it was off to a small frisk-booth for half an hour. The book had to stay there.

Every time we crossed the border together, it was like a lottery. Which of us would get through the fastest? If we wanted to stay together, then the 'winner' had nothing better to do than to wait for the 'loser' at the exit. During this 'book incident' I waited, patient at first, then puzzled, and finally quite worried. As a diversion one could make interesting observations while waiting there. East German friends and relatives greeted their loved ones with more or less extroverted enthusiasm. Starting in the eighties, East German retirees routinely received permission to visit the West. For the state there was no risk involved, because if a senior citizen didn't return, then the state had one less pension to pay. Of course, most of them did return – loaded with

Loaded with western merchandise.

western merchandise. The returnees emerged at the same exit as all others, but were processed in a separate category that we called the 'geronto line'. It was painful to observe how these old people carried heavy bags and suitcases up and down the many staircases in this labyrinth. I will never forget a little old woman limping as she carried, in addition to several bags, a standing lamp taller than herself.

When speaking of packages and old people, one has to mention the other major nuisance of this famous location: the lack of taxis. For hundreds of travelers there were just a handful of them at the station. After an hour-long crossing procedure, there could easily be an additional hour of waiting until a taxi became available. When the Wall disappeared the number of taxis increased tenfold while the price doubled. I once asked an elderly taxi driver why there used to be so few of them earlier on despite the high demand. My first guess was that the communists wanted to do away with a service that could be interpreted as a capitalist privilege of being driven around, but the man explained to me that the opposite was true. The communist regime wanted to make sure that not only rich people could take a taxi, so the taxi service was subsidized and the rides were especially cheap. A taxi driver received more money for a kilometer than the passenger paid. This way every kilometer of taxi ride from Friedrichstrasse to somebody's home cost the government money. In order to save, the administration ensured that only a few taxis were available. Surely, many old people with their heavy packages would have gladly paid twice as much in order to avoid a long wait standing on their swollen legs.

Not only the unpleasant atmosphere but also the stuffy air was a hallmark of this heavily frequented control station. One time my husband persuaded me to go with him on a visit to East Berlin. I was reluctant, but then consented and joined him on the S-Bahn to Friedrichstrasse. It was summer, the height of the tourist season. Although the border procedures took place at street level, the area was closed off from the outer world and gave the impression of a Subterranean cavern. The air inside had been largely used up by the huge crowd, and the summer heat penetrated the place enough to make it stifling. My husband took a look at the long lines for foreigners, where I was due to stand, and figured that he would have to wait an extra hour for me if we were to proceed together on the other side. I, too, was stunned by the crowd and appalled by the bad air and wasted time lying ahead. Forgetting the persuasive arguments from before, he asked me: "Didn't you say this morning that the children wanted to go to a party near Tegel lake and that you were also invited? Why don't you go, I don't mind." He didn't have to say this twice. I wished him a good time and disappeared to the lower level to take the train to my daughter's apartment in nearby Kreuzberg. She was pleasantly surprised because she suddenly had company for the long ride to Tegel.

Now that Berlin is unified, the Friedrichstrasse station is busier than ever. There are no more 'end stations' there. Train lines from the furthest southwest to the furthest northeast of the city transport masses of people, some of whom change there for other destinations. The processing cubicles have disappeared, leaving a moderate sized hallway that is merely a connecting platform between the subway and the elevated tracks. With its news and food stands, this ordinary-looking place is difficult to imagine as the intricate system of locked doors, processing windows, and frisking cabins it once was. The careful observer still discovers the one-time dividing line: there is a change in floortiles at the exit, where the processed subjects emerged into the open hallway[1] to be greeted by their waiting travel companions or East Berlin friends.

---

[1] Major reconstruction of the station in the late 1990s elimated this last trace of the control point.

"This Is Not Your Picture!"
A Night in the 'Palace of Tears'

One cannot say that we always followed the 'straight and narrow path' prescribed by East German authorities for western visitors and transit passengers. Sometimes we 'deviated from the transit routes' accidentally or deliberately.

Accidental deviations occurred, for instance, while driving from Berlin to Cologne, if one failed to notice the sign for the turnoff from the *Berliner Ring* (the expressway encircling the city) towards Hanover and proceeded south towards Leipzig. The resulting delays were always suspicious because some people would stop for unauthorized visits with relatives, meet friends at parking places along the way, or make small sightseeing tours away from the transit expressway. Depending on how long it took to notice and correct an innocent navigational error, one could only present a more-or-less 'hard luck' story at the Marienborn/Helmstedt border station.

Our first intentional deviation took place on the way from Berlin to Prague, when we couldn't resist the temptation to visit the Zwinger museum in Dresden, a beautiful Rococo building completed in 1728. It had just opened after being rebuilt from the devastation of the Second World War, and the most valuable pictures, carried away from their hiding places in 1945 as war booty, had just been returned by the Soviet Union.

We left the main road, drove into the city, whose center still had more rubble than historic buildings, and parked with our west German license plate in an inconspicuous place. We raced to the museum; ran through the gallery, glancing hurriedly right and left; and asked the way to the world-renowned *Sistine Madonna* of Raphael. After thirty seconds of rapt admiration, driven on by fear as 'transit deviants', we went on our way, but not before spending an additional five minutes in the famous clock museum.

One crime leads to another. We drove to the Czechoslovak border faster than the allowed 100 km (62.5 miles) per hour and presented our transit visa to the GDR authorities with doomsday expectations. They subtracted the starting time from our arrival time but said nothing. It happened that the second offense had canceled the first one, so we were spared the third, telling lies about losing our way.

Emboldened by this experience, my husband expressed great desire and hope to visit his home town, Frankfurt on the Oder River, which he hadn't seen for twenty years. Everybody knew that western visitors to East Berlin were forbidden to leave the city and that cars were regularly stopped for personal ID checks on the roads leading out of town. This ruled out a side trip to Frankfurt/Oder on a day excursion to the capital city of the GDR. To arrange a legal family visit was also out of the question. My husband had no relatives left there. Moreover, the red tape for these reunions was truly formidable.

An opportunity arose when we flew to Schönefeld airport from Budapest. Although general practice was that passengers with West Berlin destinations took the transit bus right away, we found no explicit rule that specified how soon one had to leave, or at which checkpoint one had to cross. Actually, our visa had this information, but we didn't look at it. My husband reasoned that because Schönefeld was outside city limits, it offered a unique starting place for a trip to Frankfurt/Oder. In a private East German car driven by his brother, we could travel inconspicuously, so through a telephone call from Budapest the next 'deviation' was plotted.

Our plane landed in mid-morning. We obtained transit visas as usual and were shown to the transit bus waiting just outside the terminal in the midst of general airport traffic. Intercepted by my brother and sister-in-law, we never reached the bus, but zoomed away by automobile towards Frankfurt/Oder. There, as in Dresden, war scars were still visible, but my husband, who had known the complete damage, saw great improvement since his departure in 1953. The cathedral had been repaired and the city hall rebuilt with its popular *Ratskeller*, a vaulted restaurant on the lower level.

In spite of the attractive setting, this restaurant was a typical representative of the GDR as a 'culinary desert'. When we were there,

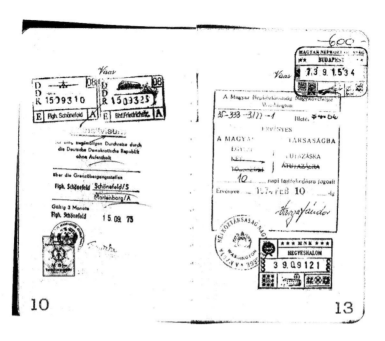

The Hungarian visa on the right shows departure by airplane
on September 15th, 1973. The GDR visa on the left shows
arrival at Schönefeld on the same day at 10 a.m., and
'deviant' exit at Friedrichstrasse minutes before midnight.

US passport photo: 'This is not your picture!'

service was almost non-existent for individual tables because a larger group of important people had their 'right-of-way'. Half an hour and some complaints later, we were given menus. It took another half an hour until a waiter came to take our order, so we had lots of time to discuss among us what to select. All in vain. Eight of the ten items on the menu weren't available. The remaining two were fish-soljanka and scrambled eggs. The first one was an eastern specialty unknown to us: a well-seasoned mixture of leftovers. Something like chop suey, odds and ends, but not necessarily from fresh ingredients. Warning lights started flashing in my mind: 'Fish leftovers are only for iron-clad stomachs, something I don't have. How old was the fish and how had it been stored?'

During the long wait before ordering, I visited the bathroom of the restaurant. In stark contrast to the well-kept dining area, it was the scene of typical communist negligence. Although Germans for many generations had had a reputation for tidiness, cleanliness, and mechanical ability, none of that was visible here. The water flowed perpetually into the toilet bowl, the door latch was hard to close and even harder to open, the warm-water tap dripped into a wash basin surrounded by dirty towels, and no toilet paper could be found. In short, the place gave a general unkept impression. All this helped me imagine the hygienic condition of the kitchen, so I ordered the scrambled eggs when my husband and brother-in-law opted for the soljanka. Needless to say, it took ages until the food came, but by that time the four of us were so hungry that everything tasted wonderful.

Seeing their old family home badly kept with peeling plaster made the brothers a little sad, but still it was for them an emotional experience to recall many fond childhood Memories. From Frankfurt our quartet proceeded to the vacation village, where my brother-in-law had just bought a weekend house. He raved how peaceful, quiet, and secluded the place was, also emphasizing that there was no chance of an ID control nearby. As we approached the area, dust clouds, engine noise, and the sound of detonations greeted us. How depressing and how dangerous! We could just imagine the headlines: 'Berlin couple brings West German and American spies to observe military maneuvers of the NVA [National People's Army]!' That would have finished us all off. We went to the weekend house, but hosts and guests were equally uneasy from the background noise and eager to leave soon.

In less than an hour we arrived in East Berlin, relieved to have made it so far, and had coffee and cake together in our relatives' apartment. Just when we wanted to leave for the checkpoint, the lunchtime soljankas started to take effect. Both men got sick and alternated running to the bathroom. I didn't say 'I told you so!' because truly I had not warned them emphatically, only mumbled that leftover fish might be dangerous. First, they probably wouldn't have listened, and second, I didn't want to act like a finicky American in the best restaurant of my husband's home town.

The four of us waited for an hour until the worst was over, then drove to the eastern side of Checkpoint Charlie. The border guard checking our papers was appalled: "You are airline passengers; what are you doing here?" Without waiting for a full answer, he sent us away. We proceeded to the Friedrichstrasse subway station, where both foreign and West German pedestrians could cross. With suitcase, briefcase, and small and big bags, my husband and I entered the control building, the 'Palace of Tears' (*Tränenpalast*). Our relatives stayed outside waiting to see if we would need further transportation to yet another destination.

With one glance at our papers, the guards put us into the 'major problem' category. They explained that the only legitimate crossing for air travelers was with the transit bus at Rudower Chaussee/ Waltersdorfer Chaussee, but by now the last bus was long gone, so it was no use going back there. Fortunately, it didn't occur to them to make us walk across the deserted airport checkpoint at night with all our baggage, so they just angrily told us to wait on a bench. We signaled to our relatives to leave, because now, no matter what, we would be spending the next few hours, if not days, in the Palace of Tears. The name derived from the sad farewells that took place at the entrance. Western relatives, visitors, or lovers had to part from their eastern counterparts and tears often flowed. In those days this glass building was connected by corridor to the train station, but it now stands alone and is used as a movie house or discotheque.

Exhausted and intimidated, we sat there for about two hours. Still, we were glad that our major wrongdoing, namely, our 'deviation' to the countryside, was not documented, just the visit to East Berlin. When the last returnees had entered the line that was to close at midnight, an officer came, reprimanded us again, but sent us into the still active control area. Luggage and all, we shuffled to the line and soon showed our airport visa and passport to a grim guard, who already knew what was wrong with us. He took a searching look at me, then at my passport, then at me, then at the passport again, then back at me – just the usual identification procedure.

But then he declared: "This is not your picture!" This 'revelation' took me by surprise, but I just shrugged my shoulders:

"What should I do, this is a bad picture of me."

I will never find out if he was really suspicious and wanted to judge from my reaction if I was traveling with false papers, or if he just wanted to be mean because I had broken a rule. The picture was indeed rather unbecoming, and retrospectively, I could interpret it as a compliment not to have been identified with it. But at midnight, dead tired in the *Tränenpalast*, I had no energy to argue and no idea what more to say, so I just stood there awaiting the next move from the officer. He saw that he couldn't make me angry or excited, so he didn't press the matter further, gave up, and let me pass.

Happily back in West Berlin, we still caught the last S-Bahn for Lichterfelde, but we made a solemn resolution never to eat fish-soljanka again and never, or hardly ever, to deviate from the transit routes.

Illegal Operation

For some years we lived in the United States, where our second daughter, Gabriella, was born in 1969. She was just as special as our first one, and we seemed to discover in her an early talent and a keen ear for music. That much greater was our shock when she brought home a letter from her nursery school pointing out a serious hearing impairment that had to be medically investigated.

From then on, pediatricians and specialists gave us ear drops, antibiotics, and advice, but there was no significant improvement. The child had frequent colds and was almost deaf in the left ear from accumulated fluid in the Eustachian tube. Implantation of a drainage tube would have been impractical, for in the winter it would have risked an infection and in the summer it would have prevented bathing in the lakes near us.

On our next visit to Germany, we were eager to show Gabriella to the ultimate expert, her Uncle Peter in East Berlin, who was *Chefarzt* (head physician) of the ear, nose, and throat department in a major hospital and a reputed surgeon in his field.

By now it was a routine matter that the family could not go over the border together, so we divided up – three to Checkpoint Charlie, one to Prinzenstrasse – and met on the other side. After greetings and a round of coffee and cake, it was time for the medical examination. Soon Uncle Peter very clearly stated the diagnosis as enlarged adenoids that had to be removed to drain the Eustachian tubes, and the sooner the better.

Of course, we wanted no one other than Peter to perform the operation, but it was easier said than done. We held the passport of the capitalist, imperialist enemy, and an operation could not be carried out in a private living room. A nose operation of this kind in those days was followed by a hospital stay of a few days until the danger of post-operative bleeding had subsided. We discussed the possibilities of an official stay, but it did not seem feasible. It would have been politically dangerous for the doctor even to ask and was probably forbidden anyway. So it had to be an illegal operation.

One of the many rules in the seventies was that West Germans visiting East Berlin for the day had to return to the West before midnight, while foreigners were allowed to stay for exactly twenty-four hours. Considering this, only I could go with Gabriella, not my husband, and the crossing point was again Checkpoint Charlie. From relatives we borrowed a car with a West Berlin license plate, and at seven-thirty in the morning on the designated day we drove up to the checkpoint. We carried only 'no-problem' presents: coffee, tea, chocolate, fruit, and brandy in permitted quantities. We stated 'family visit' as our intention, the proper name and address as the destination, and a twenty-four-hour stay as the duration. Thus there were exactly twenty-four hours for the operation and post-operative recovery.

We drove straight to the hospital. It seemed much busier than hospitals I knew in the West because of its very large out-patient traffic. There were few private practices in the GDR, but many treatment centers, most of which were also hospitals.

While asking for directions to my brother-in-law's office, I recognized that some of the personnel were part of the conspiracy while others were not. After some preliminary tests by other doctors and nurses, my brother-in-law came in for a few encouraging words. My daughter was then wheeled into the operating room, leaving me alone in the office.

To pass the time I took out a book from the bookcase and started to leaf through illustrated descriptions of terrible diseases that I had never heard of. Because on this day I had hardly any breakfast and my child was just being cut up next door under full anesthesia, the sight of these pictures made me feel like I was sailing on a stormy sea.

After some time the door opened and Peter came out with the freshly operated patient on a rolling hospital bed. Gabriella was just waking up with a whine: "It hurts very, very, very much!" Her cheeks were chalky white, while bright red blood was seeping from her nose and mouth. My brother-in-law looked at me and remarked: "I thought you were strong, otherwise I wouldn't have let you in. Please don't faint in my office!" This made some impression on me. It wasn't enough that we had involved Peter in this operation, I thought; now I am becoming an

After the illegal operation

additional medical nuisance myself. Soon my sister-in-law came and carried Gabriella to the car.

We drove the short distance between hospital and home and put the still whining child to bed. She slept most of the day and night. In the evening my sister-in-law volunteered to baby-sit. Since my brother-in-law was already home too, I went to the opera to see a ballet performed by the Hungarian State Opera Company. Afterwards I met friends from the orchestra and returned rather late with the borrowed car. It was not advisable to leave a Western car out on the street overnight because everything that could be stripped from the exterior was a collector's item. Though cars were hardly ever stolen in East Berlin, they were often partially dismantled. To avoid such a fate, I received the key of a hefty padlock that guarded a nearby yard where cars were protected from the public, though not from the elements.

There were very few street lamps in this area, and even they were rather dim, so after parking the car, I made my way to my night quarters in almost pitch blackness. Except for me, the street was completely deserted at first, but then I approached a pub from which young drunks were emerging. My main concern was my passport. What if one snatches my purse and leaves me in the outskirts of East Berlin without a passport? Am I then still an American, or do I revert to being a defector from the Eastern bloc? Would the US government get me out of here, or would the East Germans send me back to Hungary now that I had been caught behind the Iron Curtain without papers? Luckily, the drunks just wanted to reach their beds and tottered on, ignoring me with my passport and worries.

Next morning we had to get up early to observe the twenty-four-hour sojourn limit. I didn't know whether they would ask for money, lock us up, or turn us into pumpkins if we were late, but neither did I want to find out on this trip, when Gabriella was supposed to be in a hospital bed and not at the checkpoint waiting for punishment. It was not an easy drive through the morning rush hour where smelly Trabants were joined by equally smelly trucks and vans.

Little transit traffic flowed from East to West at this hour. The usual procedure was to show the personal papers at three or four places, of which the third was usually the customs examination. On the way into East Berlin the border guards were looking for contraband; on the way out, mostly for people. A slanted mirror on wheels was pushed under the car to check for any stowaways strapped there. They looked under the hood, in the trunk, and under the back seat.

In previous years, daring, small and limber people were hidden in the most impossible places. After each new escape, when a new method became public, the controls were stepped up for just that kind of hiding place. One of the most amazing and imaginative cases was a passenger who did not sit on, but hid in, the upholstery of a car seat, which is still shown in the Checkpoint Charlie Museum.

With all these precedents it was clear that everybody had to get out of the car for the 'upholstery check'. Depending on the general mood and the particular situation, the guards sometimes lifted or hand tested the back seat or asked the driver to open it up. It took a while until I learned where and how to tug on the back seat to lift it up when I got the order to do so.

The morning after the operation I told Gabriella to stay in the car lying down until I lifted her out. As the inspection of the back seat approached, I said: "The child is sick, should I lift her out?" The customs officer looked at her and either out of humanitarian consideration or fear that the pale listlessness was contagious, he answered "No" and waved us on. The operation was a success, the hearing problems disappeared, and Gabriella became a professional musician.

"Your Picture Is Wobbling!"
Penalty: One Hour and DM 20

The year 1972 brought welcome changes to border control procedures and visiting permits. From 1961 to 1972 West Germans and foreigners had been more privileged than West Berliners. West Germans and foreigners could line up at one of the checkpoints at any time and get a day visa for East Berlin, but West Berliners could do so only at special times, and even then only for seeing close relatives.

After lengthy political negotiations between the two Germanys, and with concessions on both sides, the GDR set up offices in West Berlin where all West Berliners could routinely receive day passes to visit East Berlin and even East Germany. Though the purpose and destination of the trip had to be stated, no relatives were needed. This way the West Berliners became the more privileged lot, but every crossing had to be planned ahead of time. One applied for a permit, which was to be picked up a day or two later. New crossing points opened where these 'preprocessed' candidates could pass rather speedily.

Transit traffic to and from West Germany had likewise been accelerated. One no longer had to park the car and stand for hours in alphabetically sorted columns in small barracks. One was now permitted to stay in the car while advancing through the several checking operations. The visa fee for all German transit passengers was abolished in lieu of a substantial yearly fee that the Federal Republic paid to the GDR for maintaining the transit highways. We sometimes wondered where the money went as we drove on the bumpy roads. Entry to the GDR for longer than one day still involved several weeks of red tape for everybody and was allowed only for visiting relatives or for official business.

A great change for my family was our move from the United States to West Berlin. Our unwritten 1963 marriage contract stating that we were not going to live in the divided city was set aside after my husband received a professorship at the Free University and we had the opportunity to move into the old family home five minutes away from it. My parents-in-law and grandmother-in-law had all passed away, and none of my husband's siblings could or wanted to live in the house.

At the time of our move in 1977, the cold war was by no means over. Both sides were still preparing for the ultimate confrontation; at least they kept showing their strength by generating enough war clamor to keep us awake several nights each month. The Soviets still sent supersonic jets around that broke the sound barrier near the city limits, day or night, and the Americans shelled imaginary enemy positions, preferably after midnight. Before I got used to these nightly diversions, I woke many times with a start and ran around inside the house searching for the source of the disturbing noise before realizing that the house was shaking from massive distant detonations.

Once we cut short an evening walk in the Grunewald forest after we bumped into camouflaged, armed American soldiers hidden in bushes. On another occasion, a pleasant spring afternoon, we considered a walk in the Botanical Gardens, but then decided that a walk around one of the lakes was quieter on a weekday and gave more of an out-of-the-city feeling. There were indeed only a few people walking around the lake, but the battle noise from the nearby Grunewald was so intense that we drove back to the Botanical Gardens.

After 1972, foreigners who were registered as residents in West Berlin could acquire a special ID stating their residency status, thereby giving them the same crossing rights as West Berliners of German nationality. I went to Puttkamerstrasse in Kreuzberg, where I had already spent countless hours obtaining the permit for extended stay in West Berlin (*Aufenthaltsgenehmigung*) and even a work permit. At another office in the same building I received my Berlin ID (*Berlinausweis*). Since 1962, I always had to cross the East-West divide separately, but now, after fifteen years, I could go together with my husband and children on family outings both to East Berlin and to East Germany. I became an 'amphibious' character. When friends and relatives came from abroad, I used my American passport to drive through Checkpoint Charlie. When I traveled with my husband, we passed together through a crossing point (mostly Invalidenstrasse) for West Berlin residents. Before moving to Berlin my husband and I agreed that I would never have to stand in line for the *Passierscheine* (crossing papers), a promise that he really kept. Each time we planned to visit the East, I would write a note authorizing my husband to obtain papers on my behalf. He would take this note with him along with my Berlin ID, a flimsy sheet of paper with an attached photo and a few very official stamps. Most passports and IDs are made of sturdy cardboard or plastic to withstand a certain amount of wear and tear, but this important paper was not. My husband always stuffed it into his pocket anyway with all other documents, and in the first few years it had to survive visits to cousins near Magdeburg, several performances at the East Berlin Opera, the Bertolt Brecht theater, excursions to my brother-in-law's summer cottage, some birthdays, and Christmas visits to East Berlin. First, the corners of the paper became dog-eared, then a corner of my picture got bent. Soon one of the rings attaching it to the paper came loose. Just before our next trip, I administered first aid to the abused document by ironing the corners and applying a drop of glue to the back of my picture.

The four of us, father, mother, and two children, drove up to the Invalidenstrasse crossing point en route to my brother-in-law's birthday party. We needed diverse papers, including personal IDs, visas, a list of our presents, and a list of all currency that we happened to have with us.

My husband was slightly irritated by my habit of carrying twenty Swiss francs with me all the time. I couldn't spend it, but it was 'emergency money' that could be exchanged if really needed. Each kind of money resulted in one more entry on the currency list. I also usually had US dollar bills, which allowed me to buy newspapers, books, and a hamburger or a hot dog (before I turned vegetarian) at the American army stores at Truman Plaza in Zehlendorf. The children had counted the money in their pockets as well, and my husband handed the whole stack of papers to the guard. After careful inspection, in which ears and noses on the pictures were matched with their originals, the guard pointed to my carefully doctored ID: "Your picture is wobbling! This document is not valid! Park the car and come into the office!"

'Good grief,' I thought, 'here goes the next hour, the coffee will get cold and the cake soggy!' My time estimate turned out to have been rather accurate. I entered the office barrack and waited alone in the corridor. After a while, somebody appeared with a Polaroid camera, commanded me to look straight ahead, and took my picture. His grim manner was more funny than threatening, and as my deadly serious picture slid out of the camera, I had the urge to both laugh and cry. After another half hour of inaction an officer typed up my personal data with one finger, and the newly developed picture was firmly attached to the paper. I received an *Identitätsbescheinigung*, meaning proof of personal identity. This was a great favor considering that I had arrived with an invalid document, thus with 'uncertain' identity. The picture cost DM 10, the paper another DM 10, and I was told that this temporary ID was only valid for this crossing. For next time, I would have to have a new Berlin ID and it had better be in good condition. When I returned to the car, both children had red eyes and were still sobbing. Their vivid imaginations had run away with them. In their mind's eye, they had seen me being tortured behind closed doors. My husband told them that this was nonsense, but shortly before the hour was up, he also started to wonder in what way I was getting processed.

Not all foreign residents flocked to get their Berlin IDs. In fact few knew that this possibility existed at all. Since the bureau at Puttkamer-strasse wasn't one of my favorite places, I long postponed getting the new ID. I either went separately to East Berlin with my passport or developed a headache or stomachache just in time for the next family visit. This wasn't even simulation; I did feel rather sick if I thought of the long waits at any of the processing stations.

Finally, Johann Sebastian Bach brought me to Puttkamerstrasse for my new document in 1985. To my surprise, most of the other patiently waiting foreigners there were also fans of his: people seeking to take advantage of the only relatively easy way to go to Leipzig and hear one or other of the several musical events celebrating the 300th birthday of the composer. I was lucky to have gotten reserved tickets to the St. Matthew Passion in the *Thomaskirche* of Leipzig, an opportunity that could not be passed up just because my picture was loose on my old ID. I received a brand new, but still flimsy, sheet of paper with a friendly photo and invested right away in a fitting plastic cover to prolong its life.

This important document served me until the day of the monetary union of East and West Germany on July 1st, 1990. In those last months of the GDR's existence, Berliners and Berlin residents could come and

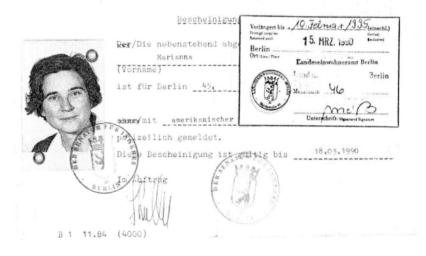

This Berlin ID (Berlinausweis or Senatsbescheinigung) gave a foreign citizen crossing rights as a West Berliner. Between December 1989 and July 1st, 1990, one could enter and leave the GDR free of charge by just waving this sheet of paper. The document expired in March 1990 and was extended until 1995, but it had no use after German unification.

go by just waving their IDs, whereas foreigners were still required to cross at designated points[1] and pay the visa fee each time.

---

[1] The controls on traffic between East and West Germany, including Berlin, stopped on July 1st, 1990, the day of monetary union. The GDR itself did not cease to exist until October 3rd, 1990, the day of unification.

Body Search Before *Parsifal*

Time and again we faced the question of whether or not a cultural excursion to East Berlin would be worth the trouble of the border crossing there and back. Optimists believed that the controls would be light and the performance beautiful; pessimists thought otherwise. Actually, some people reported difficult times at the crossing points more often than others. After being processed, several people noticed that their personal documents bore mysterious dots, put there with a ball point pen. These markings could not be accidental and it was assumed that they were secret codes of the GDR state security agency (*Stasi*, short for *Staatssicherheit*). The best way to get rid of them was probably to get a new passport.

The border personnel wore either the uniform of the NVA (National People's Army) or of the GDR customs service, but actually the officers all belonged to a special unit of the Stasi (secret police), called *Pass und Fahndung* (Passport and Investigation).[1]

In the early seventies, during our stay in the United States, my husband renewed his passport at the German Consulate in Detroit, Michigan. Something on that passport wasn't to the liking of the GDR officials, so even after the 1972 acceleration of processing procedures, on account of the new rules worked out by the East and West German authorities, we had to park the car at the transit control points while the guards 'meditated' over his passport for an unduly long time without ever giving an explanation. All such delays disappeared when we

---

[1] The West Germans used to call all border officials '*Vopos*', short for *Volkspolizisten* (People's Policemen), but this designation was incorrect. The real *Vopos* were policemen inside the GDR. They directed traffic and fined or arrested people for all kinds of trespasses. The border guards were not members of the *Volkspolizei*.

moved to Berlin in 1977 and my husband received his new personal documents as a West Berlin resident. He also obtained a new West German passport, but it was 'taboo' to carry it while crossing into East Berlin.

According to West German law, West Berliners of German nationality were citizens of the German Federal Republic (*Bundesrepublik*), while the Soviet Union and other Eastern-bloc countries insisted that West Berlin was a self-governed extra-territorial entity under allied supervision. As the Communists saw it, the inhabitants didn't have the right to carry a West German passport, only their 'provisional' (*behelfsmässiger*) personal ID. If a West Berliner was subjected to a 'pocket check' at one of the crossing points and a West German passport came to light, the person was simply sent back. The opposite was true for West Germans. Since West Germany proper was considered a foreign country, its citizens *had* to show their passports while transiting the German Democratic Republic.

A West Berlin personal ID and a West German one looked almost identical; only the word 'provisional' and the color distinguished them from each other. A joke making the rounds at the time had it that a Bavarian policeman helping out in a crowd control unit at a rock concert in West Berlin looked at the personal ID of a young Berliner and asked: "This is a provisional ID, when do you get your final one?" Most West Germans didn't know about the two million provisional IDs in West Berlin and were also oblivious to the fact that they needed a passport to go there. Some of them found out the hard way when they were not allowed to cross the border without one. Many West Germans did not have a passport, and it was an oddity that they could visit all of western Europe with their personal ID but could not visit or transit East Germany.

Between Hanover and Berlin, I once traveled with a young couple who had applied for a passport for the first time in their lives just to visit West Berlin. Before the border they were contemplating whether their virginal passports would get a stamp or two on this exotic trip. As a seasoned traveler, I assured them that after their round-trip journey they would surely carry home four colorful stamps. They were genuinely happy when the first 'foreign' stamp landed in their passports. For me it was amazing to realize that both Germanys had managed to bring up a generation of young people who regarded the other half of their parents' one-time homeland as an exotic foreign country. West Berlin residents, young and old, German and foreign, had a much closer view of East-West realities, especially if they had relatives on the other side or if they wanted to participate in the cultural life of their eastern neighbor. There were rich opportunities for finding good theater, opera, and concert performances on both sides of the Wall. Both Berlins were showcases for their respective countries, and just as the American moon landing had been fueled by the competition with the Soviet Union, the capitalist and communist systems constantly had to demonstrate to each other their superiority in supporting and producing cultural events. Bonn was very generous in financing a great number of theaters, operas, and orchestras in West Berlin, and the GDR put in equal effort to keep up high standards in East Berlin. Musicians and actors think back nostalgically to the days when these subsidies were almost unlimited. Since unification, the East-West competition has ended; the city has too many duplicate companies and too little money to finance them all.

Westerners were encouraged to attend eastern performances, but the obstacles in getting to them could be considerable. One needed luck to obtain tickets, because they were mostly sold in factories and offices to those working there. The box office had few leftovers. We once had the offer from one of my husband's students to get five tickets for a gala performance of Richard Wagner's *Parsifal*. This opera is endlessly long, and adding another hour to cross the border there and back made the evening even longer. We took the S-Bahn to Friedrichstrasse and fortunately managed to arrive at the State Opera (*Staatsoper*) well before starting time.

The other couple in our party also arrived soon after us, so we waited together for Michael K. – the student – to show up with the tickets. Our companions started to be uneasy when the first bell rang, and we joined them in nervousness when the second bell sounded. Soon the last members of the audience hurried inside, but Michael was still not in sight. We had already given up on hearing the prelude, but we still nourished a vague hope of being admitted before the first act got under way. At the last possible moment, Michael arrived ghostly white, but still breathless from running. With little time for explanations, we just got the message of a 'nightmare' at the crossing.

During the generously long intermission Michael could be more

Michael in the frisking cabin, while four people are waiting
for their opera tickets.

specific and related how he had arrived at the Friedrichstrasse control point in good time, but had been asked to wait. In a dark suit and a tie, with opera tickets for that evening in his pocket, his destination couldn't have been clearer. Still the agents asked endless questions about his plans and contacts. He only told the plain truth that four people from West Berlin were waiting for him and for the tickets. No mercy. More waiting followed and finally came the command to undress in a frisking cabin. Naked, he was just as innocent as in his evening attire and, except for the five tickets, nothing of value was found on him. Finally, the procedure ended and he hastily tied his tie without a mirror and rushed to the opera. Now it became clear to him that he was a chronically 'suspicious' character in the eye of the Stasi. He also discovered a mysterious ball point pen dot behind the upper right corner of his picture, a mark to which he attributed the repeated long delays in his Processing. The climax was this body search before *Parsifal.*

Even a glass of champagne during the second intermission and a good performance didn't restore my mood. The poor air circulation in the opera house, the full auditorium, and a big crowd on the stage in the last act, mixed with the thought of the crowd awaiting us in the airless control area at Friedrichstrasse, gave me the feeling of suffocation, a kind of panic attack that almost forced me to leave. For me the final words of the opera about redemption (*Erlösung*) this time meant some fresh air and a speedy return to West Berlin.

Schönefeld Blues: On Foot to the Airport

As a four-power city, Berlin had four military airports, three of which also served civilian air passengers. The American military airport, Tempelhof, famed for the historic airlift in 1948-49, was also the western civilian air terminal until the French airbase in Tegel, built up into a larger, more comfortable airfield, replaced it in 1975. Until 1990, only American, British, and French airplanes were allowed to land in West Berlin, a very favorable deal for some airlines and unfavorable for others. The British airport, Gatow, mentioned only when a member of the royal family landed there, had no civilian flights.

Schönefeld was the Russian military airport just outside the Berlin city limits, close to the Wall. It also served the capital city of the GDR and had considerable international air traffic. Most of all, it was the hub of Interflug, the East German national airline. At the same time, the West German giant, Lufthansa, could not land anywhere in Berlin.

Routes to several capital cities were shared equally by Interflug and the national airline of the particular country. Direct flights to Helsinki, Vienna, and Budapest were only possible from Schönefeld. I considered it a lucky break if I could fly Finnair, Austrian Airlines, or Malév, and an unlucky one if I had to take Interflug. My anti-Interflug attitude was not based on prejudice but primarily on 'the smell' in its airplanes.

All visitors to the GDR knew the characteristic, pervasive smell of a certain disinfectant used in all public places. Each Interflug baggage compartment was so hygienically saturated with this substance that all clothing had to be washed before one could comfortably wear it again. I jokingly 'patented' the idea of putting everything into tightly closed plastic bags before placing them in a suitcase. Of course, this couldn't be done for one's nose, or for what one wore.

Two anecdotes from one round-trip with Interflug to Vienna illustrate the attitude of others. Just before departure from Schönefeld, 'the smell' intensified when the doors of the plane were closed. Suffering, I remarked to my neighbor, "Isn't this smell terrible?"

"What smell?" he asked. It turned out that he was on tour as a member of the Dresden Opera orchestra. I tried to explain which smell I meant, to which he, in turn, explained that since the chemical was everywhere, he was used to it and it didn't bother him at all.

Boarding in Vienna for the return flight, I noticed that the disinfectant hadn't been refilled to full strength. Since the doors of the airplane were still open, there was only a mild whiff. Two Viennese women entered and started to sniff around. In a loud, excited conversation they made the observation that there was a terrible odor and one had to alert the personnel because something must be leaking. When the women sat down near me, I couldn't resist enlightening them about 'the smell' as a national characteristic of the GDR. Telling them of the musician from Dresden, I warned them that on their return trip the odor would become much stronger, but consoled them that the offending chemical wasn't as lethal as their noses would have them believe at first sniff, so their chances for survival were good.

Most passengers from West Berlin took the transit bus from the *Funkturm* (Radio Tower) bus terminal to Schönefeld airport. The trip took at least an hour, sometimes more, depending on the traffic in West Berlin and the duration of two usually lengthy border checks. At the Waltersdorfer Chaussee exit, the western police had lists of terrorists or drug dealers, and probably each of us was screened against these lists. Suspicious characters had to leave the bus and enter a booth, prompting the rest of the passengers to glance nervously at their watches.

The relief felt when we were finally moving again evaporated a hundred yards further when we stopped at the eastern checkpoint. An East German officer climbed aboard with his typical 'tummy desk'. This was a box hanging by a strap from the neck and just covering the stomach. When opened, the front of the box formed a horizontal platform, where transit-visa forms could be filled out and energetically stamped. The passenger received the original, and the copy was filed in one of the pockets of the 'tummy desk' for further reference. After everybody had been supplied with a visa, the bus had only a few minutes' drive to the air terminal, where the passengers disembarked and mingled with the rest of the crowd on their way to the check-in counters.

This arrangement was changed in the mid-eighties either to speed up the traffic, which until then had been held up by the seemingly interminable tummy-desk ritual, or to isolate the westerners from the natives. With the new procedure the bus stopped at the checkpoint only to pick up one or two hours before flight time. If the bus was full, one could get on the next one an hour later and perhaps still make it to the airport one hour before departure. There was another scheduled stop halfway to the airport at the Tempelhof S-Bahn station, but the bus only stopped if it still had empty seats. If not, then it zoomed by the waiting passengers, not informing them verbally about their tough luck. In high season, chances were at best fifty-fifty that the next bus would have more room than the previous one. I first thought that this stop was only for optimists with good nerves and enough money for a taxicab to the airport, but after seeing people standing there wildly gesticulating in the hope that the bus driver would pick them up if he saw that they wanted to get on, I rather suspected that these passengers were simply unaware of the conditional nature of this stop.

My husband, an efficient person who didn't like to waste time, happily anticipated a great speed-up when West Berliners were allowed to park at Schönefeld during round-trip air travel from there. Trying this out for the first time, we left home only an hour and a half before flight time, went through the controls, parked the car, and walked to the check-in area. A stewardess at the desk informed us in a cool manner that we could turn back because the passengers for our flight to Vienna had been checked in already. It was still thirty-five minutes until departure. Long argumentation, pleading, and promises that we would never be that tardy again made her open the door beside the check-in desk, where the last of the Vienna passengers were still waiting in front of the metal detectors.

Another time, in 1983, I was on my way to Vienna for the nineteenth birthday of my daughter, Charlotte, loaded with presents, household articles, food and clothing. Instead of taking the transit bus, I accepted another of my husband's great time-saving ideas. He suggested driving me to the airport on his way to his brother's weekend house, which was sixteen miles outside East Berlin. With his proper day pass (*Passierschein*) and my airline ticket we set out on our next Schönefeld adventure.

The inspection on the west side took only seconds, but long rows of cars were lined up in front of the eastern checkpoint. These were divided into airport traffic, West Berliners visiting the GDR, and GDR returnees. (West Germans and foreigners were allowed to use this crossing point only in conjunction with a valid airplane ticket.) A guard looked into our mixed destination papers and showed us to the longest and slowest line. After considerable waiting and little headway, my husband thought that it would be better for me to walk through the pedestrian queue and for him to take another checkpoint, like Invalidenstrasse further north in the city. From our car we could see *Barkas* minibuses coming and going every ten to fifteen minutes, taking passengers to the airport. As I approached the pedestrian control window, only a few people were in front of me. The guard who had instructed us on which line to wait in jumped in front of me and shouted: "What are you doing here? Go back to your car!" This sudden attack startled me. I confessed that there was no car to go back to because my husband had left to try his luck at another checkpoint. The tall officer had a frightening appearance with hollow cheeks, yellow teeth, and a generally unhealthy look that suggested excessive alcohol and nicotine consumption, maybe a stomach or liver ailment, and a mean disposition. He flew into a rage and quickly found the right penalty for not following his instructions.

"You came to the checkpoint in a car, and now I am going to make sure that you don't take the limousine reserved for pedestrians. You have to go on foot to the airport!"

Sure enough, the officer held me up when I could have boarded the minibus with a small group of people all provided with transit visas. The driver, seeing me with all my bags ready for the ride, waited for a while, but my tormentor ordered him to depart, leaving me behind. I firmly resisted showing distress and thus giving him further sadistic pleasure. Holding my head high and my body asstraight as I could while pulling one suitcase and carrying two heavy bags, I walked away from the checkpoint.

At the corner of the main road to the airport, finally out of my persecutor's sight, I started to hitchhike. One Trabant after another passed, but didn't stop. I probably looked too western and too 'irregular'. Everyone knew that it was forbidden for GDR citizens to help West Germans on the transit routes. Fortunately, a West Berlin

I firmly resisted showing distress.

couple soon picked me up and drove me to the airport. Nervous and exhausted, I hurried to the check-in counter, where to my relief a few passengers were still lined up. I didn't have to plead for mercy like the last time, and kept my promise that I would never be tardy again.

Constant Money Problems:
"Don't Pay Me, I Pay You!"

A family visit to East Berlin or East Germany was not a cheap excursion. In the last years of the Wall's existence, every grown-up had to exchange DM 25 per person. With two grown children, a family of four had to spend the considerable sum of DM 100 just to see relatives for an afternoon of coffee and cake. Of course, this money was not simply taken away. At an exchange rate of one to one, visitors to the GDR received East Marks to be given out at 'one's heart's desire'. This exchanged money had to be spent to the last *Pfennig* (penny) because taking eastern money over the border was strictly prohibited and because converting the cash obtained in this 'compulsory exchange' (*Zwangsumtausch*) back into West German marks was not possible. This way, the capitalist visitors were forced to spend liberally in the GDR, although this was easier said than done.

Spending the East German money in a restaurant was a possibility, but without a reservation, one either couldn't get a table or had to wait forever to be seated. Service used to be extremely slow, and it was impossible to eat 25 East Marks worth of food at one sitting anyway. Buying groceries at a food store was no solution to spending exchange money either, because one wasn't allowed to export the food to the West. Consumer goods like clothing or household items were seldom attractive in quality or price, and, as with food, some items were not exportable.

Visitors with cars would have liked to take gasoline, but a western car was allowed to fill up only at special stations and only for DM. A 'family loophole' was to park the western car around the corner from a gas station and to send an eastern nephew with a gasoline can to buy five liters of gasoline and have him pour it into the gas tank. The procedure could be repeated either at the same or at another station, but

An effective way to get rid of money.

it was tedious and dangerous.

We were willing to give the exchange money to our relatives, but they didn't want to receive such 'handouts' and rather helped us preserve our East-Mark riches. The only permissible and worthwhile items to purchase were books and sheet music. When our children were still only playing beginner's pieces, we bought advanced solo and chamber music pieces for piano and strings, most of them published by Edition Peters in Leipzig. One didn't buy what one needed, but what was available. More than two decades of exchange money resulted in a valuable music library, so our children had to continue their music education to 'grow into' this accumulated treasure.

On shorter visits money had to be spent quickly. My husband once came to pick me up from Schönefeld airport by car. The customs officer noticed at the return trip that he spent less than one hour in the East and asked: "Do you have money of the GDR with you?" He realized that the untouched 25 East Marks was still in his pocket and confessed his sin.

The situation was critical, and he asked helplessly: "How can I get rid of this money?" The officer recommended the Red Cross collection box in another building nearby. My husband left the car in search of the Red Cross. On his return he announced that the transaction had taken place, but later told me that he had only found a locked door and had put the money on the steps.

Another time, two eastern visits took place in short succession, and the remaining funds from the first visit were successfully hidden under a stone in a park. We found the money and spent it during the second visit. An inelegant, but effective way to get rid of money is to throw it away. Approaching the Invalidenstrasse crossing point shortly before midnight, we realized that we still had GDR money with us. To avoid losing any time, we rolled down the car windows and when nobody was to be seen, threw out a mark or two at a time until we were light and legal for the return trip.

One was allowed to open a savings account, but our visiting days happened to be mostly on weekends, when banks were closed. Sometimes we planned ahead and carried an envelope and GDR postage stamps to send remaining paper money to our relatives in East Berlin, but the coins had to be disposed of otherwise. Once, my husband was driving late at night on the deserted streets of East Berlin and saw a hitchhiker who had just missed the last bus home. The rules

West Berliners watch as the windows of East Berlin apartments are walled up in 1961. The facade of this house, Bernauer Strasse 48, happend to be part of the East-West border.

First-generation wall blocking the entrance to the Church of Reconciliation, Bernauer Strasse, 1961.

*Second-generation wall under construction in 1963,
Bernauer Strasse.*

*The third-generation wall was ideally suited for grafitti, here at
Potsdamer Platz in 1984.*

The subway and train station Friedrichstrasse in 1974.

The `Palace of Tears`, connected on the left by a passage to the Friedrichstrasse station.

Cars leaving West Berlin at the control point
Dreilinden/Drewitz in 1972.

Fifteen years later: extended `deluxe` version
of the same location.

Transit road entering East German territory on the way to
Schönefeld Airport.

Invalidenstrasse crossing point for West Berlin residents.

*Prinzenstrasse/Heinrich-Heine-Strasse crossing point
for West Germans.*

The wall separated the East German village Nieder Neuendorf from its waterfront for twenty-eight years.

The ultimate wall experience: secluded path in Steinstücken, a small community surrounded by the wall.

Road leading to Steinstücken walled in on both sides.

The narrowest death strip (6 meters) around Steinstücken with watchtower and lamps.

A view from the Brandenburg Gate (East Berlin) towards the Reichstag (on the left in West Berlin)

The Wall around the Brandenburg Gate. The wide, flat segment on the right side of the picture became the `dance wall` in November 1989.

The death strip viewed from a watchtower near Potsdamer Platz. The house on the left is Stresemannstrasse 128 in East Berlin.

A view along Niederkirchner Strasse. On the left is Gropiusbau (a museum in West Berlin), on the right is Niederkirchner Strasse 3-5 (East Berlin). Since 1993 this building is the House of Representatives for the city-state (Bundesland) Berlin.

The Church of Reconcilation is blown up in 1985.
The walled-up houses had been torn down
several years before.

Empty space left by the demolished Church of Reconciliation.
The houses on the right are on the West Berlin side of
Bernauer Strasse. The house on the left is Strelitzer Strasse 50
in East Berlin.

*Looking south, this GDR archive photo shows the entrance to the
Checkpoint Charlie control area, later the site of the C.C.
Business Center. In the background is West Berlin.*

*Warming up for the evening concert, Canadian pianist Jon Kimura
Parker tries his skill as 'wallpecker' on December 3, 1989.*

The allied control booth at Checkpoint Charlie is lifted away on June 22, 1990, in the presence of foreign ministers and other politicans.

that easterners were not allowed to ride in western cars and that eastern cars were not allowed to pick up western hitchhikers were automatically, if unofficially, null and void when it was dark and nobody could observe the violation. My husband picked up the young man and drove him to his doorstep, which happened to be not too great a detour on the way to the border-crossing station. The young man was very grateful and wanted to pay two marks as taxi fare. This reminded my husband that he still had five East Marks in his pocket and pleaded: "Don't pay me, but let me give you the rest of my exchange money!" The young man was first embarrassed and protested at taking money from a stranger, but then he understood that this was rather a favor and accepted it. Thus he had a lucky night: door-to-door free taxi service and a tip of five marks!

Turkish Bazaar at the Checkpoint, Supermarket in the Trunk

Tedious waiting for processing was the hallmark of all the East-West checkpoints, but Checkpoint Charlie and Dreilinden stand out in my mind as having consumed a not insignificant fraction of my lifetime. In the 1980s, the processing at Checkpoint Charlie had been reduced to the actual checking of documents and possessions if the traffic was light and if no 'problem cases' showed up just ahead in the line.

My Uncle George from America came to visit in 1979, and as a part of sightseeing and introduction to family members, he wanted to visit East Berlin. Friends of his at the US embassy in Bonn offered to arrange a ride in a military jeep that could zoom through Checkpoint Charlie without controls under the four-power treaty. Although Uncle George detested waiting around, he declined the generous offer as unnecessary extra treatment and elected to have me as his chauffeur and guide to East Berlin. The entry took about an hour because of the long line of cars ahead of us, but I was partially successful at keeping Uncle George entertained with my stories and questions about his work and travels.

The way back was a nightmare for an impatient person. Just ahead of us, in a station wagon with West Berlin license plates, sat a Turkish family consisting of father, mother, grandma, and four children, probably returning from a vacation in Turkey. The customs agents wanted to inspect the space under their back seat and the bottom of their trunk. For this procedure, all of them had to get out and remove dozens of bags and heaps of loose objects. Children's equipment, food, pillows, blankets, rugs, pots, and pans gradually surrounded their car. The mother held the baby; the grandmother was too old to do anything but admonish the three small children running around. The 'halo' of colorful merchandise encircling the car reminded me of a Turkish bazaar.

All my efforts to placate my uncle failed, and he repeated several times: "If I had only accepted the offer from the embassy!" and, "Who would have thought that this would take so long!" or "This is pure harassment!"

Worse yet, packing their belongings back into the station wagon proved to take even longer than the unpacking had. It was hard to believe that the whole 'bazaar' could fit into the vehicle, and indeed, the nervous and hurried repacking hardly left any room for the passengers. Our checking went rather quickly and uneventfully, but I couldn't console Uncle George, who still fumed for days when telling about his terrible time at the checkpoint.

Probably most West Berliners remember Dreilinden as the place of endless rows of cars and hours of delay on their trips out of the city. At the start of school vacations, the number of bumper-to-bumper cars topped the largest accumulation of vehicles I have ever seen anywhere. The backup would even flood city streets near the Dreilinden/Drewitz checkpoint, causing hopeless snarls that sometimes cut off access to the Wannsee district in southwest Berlin.

By the 1980s this control point had expanded to about eight parallel lanes in each direction and numerous booths. A covered conveyor belt carried the documents from one checking officer to the other further up the queue. Lights flooded the checkpoint in the evening, and this booming 'business' seemed to be constructed for eternity.

Imagine the air, with eight columns of a hundred cars each inching along, the processed members steadily replenished by new arrivals. To avoid suffocation it became the custom to push the cars instead of starting the engine for each advance. Still, there were always enough weak people in heavy cars to ensure a constant high concentration of exhaust fumes.

The 'tin avalanche' (*Blechlawine*) branched into smaller rivers. Transit traffic to West Germany constituted the largest branch, followed by transit to Poland; while the traffic volume in the lane for 'entry into the GDR' swelled up only before holidays. This category included GDR returnees, one-day visitors, longer visitors, and business travelers.

The transit travelers sometimes had to wait for hours to get to the control booths, but the 'entry' traffic suffered by far the longer processing per car. My husband hated waiting but loved the surroun-

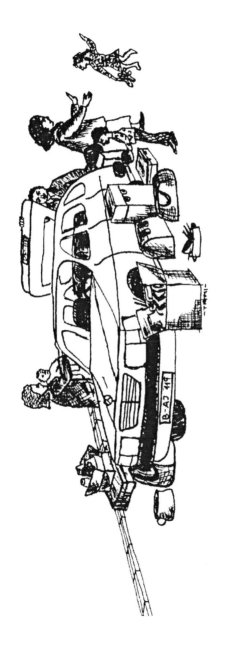

Bazaar at the checkpoint.

ding land, the beautiful lakes, dense forests, tree-lined country roads, and the palaces and parks of Potsdam. Not only the length but the atmosphere of the border procedures depressed me every time, and an excursion had to be very special to compensate for the inconvenience.

We had already lived in Berlin for several years when my husband finally persuaded me to see Potsdam and the palace of Sanssouci. Keeping his promise that I would never have to go to the *Passierschein* office, he had to collect all the necessary papers. The weather happened to be terrible on the chosen day, but my husband, a good salesman for his favorite projects, told me that the pouring rain was to our advantage because the border crossing would be almost empty. We joined the 'GDR entry' lane at Dreilinden and talked about the great dinner that we would eat to spend at least part of the mandatory exchange of DM 25 per person. The upset stomach of Frankfurt/Oder almost a decade earlier had already been forgotten. We had heard of a good restaurant in a new hotel, and since it was early we would surely get a table.

There were not too many cars in the line, but they progressed at a snail's pace. Directly ahead of us a woman drove a Mercedes with a small child in the back seat. The guard signaled that it was their turn. The checking of the papers went normally, and then came customs clearance with the usual command: "Open your trunk!" The woman obeyed, and to everybody's amazement, a small supermarket of goods came to light. Canned and fresh fruit, sausages, cheeses, bottles of juice and liquor, sweets, coffee, tea, and detergents. None of these items were individually forbidden, just the total quantity. Some discussion followed that we couldn't hear and then an energetic arm swing: "Come into the control booth!" She followed the officer and left the small girl, about five years old, in the car. The child sensed that something was wrong and started whimpering, then crying. Shortly after, she began screaming bloody murder. I had the urge to go talk to her, but of course it wasn't me she needed, but her mother. Furthermore, moving into the control area without permission was forbidden and the trunk was still open. How could I explain that I was leaving my car to give the child psychological assistance and not to steal or conceal goods from the 'supermarket'. This heartbreaking scene seemed to last forever, and I blamed myself for not doing anything. We never found out how the confrontation ended, for when the mother came out she had to park the car and her ordeal continued. My appetite was gone for the planned dinner, but my husband already had the solution: "We have lost so much time that we will not get a table anyway."

Soon it was our turn for customs: "Open your trunk!" Nothing in it, just a first-aid kit and trash.

"You didn't fill out the customs declaration!"

My husband: "We are not carrying any presents."

"No coffee, tea, alcohol?"

"Nothing, we are only going sightseeing to Potsdam."

This made us seem especially suspicious. Could it be that a couple would go through all the red tape, all the tedious waiting, pay DM 50 exchange money, just to see a palace and a park in pouring rain? Now they really wanted to see what we had to conceal! The commands came like machine-gun fire:

"Lift out your back seat; take out the rubber floormats; open the glove compartment, ashtray, and hood; show the space under the spare tire!" I had a hard time swallowing the tears of laughter while my husband was unearthing more and more of the litter that had accumulated during his boating vacation in France. He apologized when two rotten apple cores and a moldy piece of cheese surfaced, and my amusement rose when he helplessly looked around for a waste-basket in which to deposit the offending objects. The situation became dramatic when he turned up French small change that was not on the currency declaration he had filled out. My husband argued that he had just returned from France and the money had accidentally come to rest in its hidden place not on purpose. How does a border guard feel to see fresh trash from France, a place that normal GDR citizens had no hope of ever visiting? In any case, the officer kept his stony expression throughout the whole comic procedure. Finally convinced that we were really crazy enough to endure all this nuisance just for a few hours of sightseeing, he allowed us to proceed.

We drove to the restaurant and, as we had expected, didn't get in. All tables were already occupied, and a long line of people was waiting for the second seating, not sure if they would still get a table or food in this economy of scarcity. The same hotel had a café where, still too early for the afternoon customers, we got coffee and good cake. This hardly made a dent in our East-Mark riches, so at Sanssouci we bought several guide books and postcards.

The controls on the return trip were much lighter, and the small mirror pushed under the car didn't reveal any hidden passengers, so in a few minutes we advanced to the last step. Still in his 'sales-talk' mood, my husband remarked cheerily that the return controls were really light and in two more minutes we would be in WestBerlin. It had just crossed my mind not to praise the day before the evening, when a loud shot rang through the air. All the booms of the control area lowered at once and the processing stopped. Several *Barkas* minibuses sped away and everybody looked intently in the direction of the shot. Fifteen minutes later the vehicles came back, but nothing unusual was visible and no explanations were provided. Did a rabbit trigger a mine on the death strip? Did someone fire a warning shot? Perhaps someone shot another person dead? The whole depressing reality of the Wall came to our mind, and when the booms finally opened we drove home in shocked silence.

"Don't Worry, I Have All the Papers!" (Except for One)

The border between the two Germanys was guarded in equal parts by weapons and bureaucracy. Recently, I listened to a heated argument in which an East and a West Berliner, both of whom had lived through all twenty-eight years of the Wall, were trying to decide who had had a harder time going on vacation by car with a large family. The East Berliner said that the Westerners could go wherever they wanted, and showing personal papers at the transit points was only a minor inconvenience. The Westerner argued to the contrary that the transit procedure posed a major inconvenience, a real hardship, adding that Easterners could drive without obstacles, at least within their own country. In my opinion, the long waiting hours, constant stress, and mishaps with the paperwork did reduce the quality of life. The feeling of elation while driving or walking unhindered through the earlier sites of border obstacles also proves retrospectively how oppressed one usually felt there before the Wall fell.

My family can look back on a long string of hardships, some of which were caused or aggravated by our chaotic habits in dealing with papers. In a strict bureaucracy, the fetish of 'paper' has to be respected, and the right one, in good condition, presented at the right place and at the right time. We failed miserably on all counts. First we couldn't agree whether it was better for one person to have all the papers or whether every passenger should scrounge around in his or her own pockets, briefcase or handbag when the time came to present them. A centralized 'family-document administration' initiated and chaired by me proved to be very efficient at the border.

One day, however, my husband was about to board a flight from Tegel airport to Bonn when he discovered that his personal ID[1] was still

---

[1] Because the papers of travelers crossing the border from East to West Berlin were not examined systematically by Western officials, any foreigner could

with me at home, so I got demoted from administrator to inspector. Every time we were leaving for a trip I called out, imitating the rough voice of the East German guards: "*Passkontrolle!*" (passport inspection) and checked if everybody in our party had the necessary documents (car registration, driver's license, passport or personal ID , and crossing papers). During one such check my husband couldn't find his driver's license just before we were to leave for Cologne, so he had to endure my driving on the transit route in East Germany. On the West German stretch, between Helmstedt and Cologne, where the penalty for driving without one's license was calculable, he took over the wheel.

On yet another occasion, my husband obtained the relevant crossing papers (*Passierscheine*) for himself and for me in preparation for my brother-in-law's fiftieth birthday in East Berlin. We allotted half an hour for driving to the border, another thirty minutes for crossing, and an additional half an hour for navigating in East Berlin, including some time to get lost in our never-ending attempt to find a shortcut. Before leaving the house, the 'inspector' called out loud: "*Passkontrolle!*" and wanted to see the documents one by one. My husband disarmed me in a convincing manner: "Don't worry, I have all the papers!" and lifted a wad of documents that looked bulky enough to contain everything. We were eager to leave to get to the party on time because we had a bad record for punctuality with the two brothers and one sister, who were all to be present that afternoon.

While driving to the border we recalled some of our abortive attempts to get to our relatives on time. When we lived in Cologne and my brother-in-law Ulrich in Bonn, we established our reputation for lateness, but once, when we truly left on time, a flat tire made us especially late and very dirty. My husband showed his greasy hands and told the hard-luck story to his brother, but Ulrich remarked: "Anybody could say that!"

We were deeply hurt by his lack of confidence in us. Sister Sabine, who lived in West Berlin, also found out that we couldn't be punctual

---

enter West Berlin without carrying a valid visa for West Germany. All passengers therefore underwent a thorough check of personal documents by the West Berlin police before boarding an airplane at Tegel airport.

Waiting for papers

even when we tried hard. My husband told her the true, but somewhat incredible, story that he had gotten lost en route to her house. Leaving the city expressway (*Stadtring*) near the radio tower (*Funkturm*) junction, he accidentally took the Avus expressway leading south, which led us back almost to where we had come from.

Against the background of these fateful failures to be punctual, my husband cheerfully asserted: "Today we're sure to get there on time. There is hardly any traffic at the border!" We pulled to a stop at the control point Invalidenstrasse, and he presented the impressive heap of documents to the guard, who carefully opened and held them in the prevailing stormy wind. The officer turned each paper around, searched through the heap a second time, and asked: "Where is your green multiple visa card [*Mehrfachvisum*]?" Pale and shaken, my husband turned to me with the words, "I am going back home; I left it on the shelf in the hallway." He took the documents back from the guard and backed up the car to leave the control point. I had a bad conscience. What kind of an 'inspector' was I to let such a mistake happen? As a consolation, my husband dropped me off at the national gallery (*Nationalgalerie*), drove home alone, and picked me up on the second approach to the border. We estimated this pick-up time too optimistically, and I remember waiting outside the museum in a freezing wind and laying the foundations of a bad cold. We arrived almost an hour late at the birthday party, but nobody was very surprised. They knew that brother Burk always came late; the only thing that ever changed was the explanation.

Another episode of self-inflicted stress happened at the transit checkpoint Dreilinden/Drewitz when I was driving with my two daughters to Hanover, where my husband planned to meet us. We were already inching our way toward the first passport control point in an endless row of cars when I exclaimed "The car paper!" It had just occurred to me that one couldn't drive through this checkpoint without showing the vehicle registration card, and that this card might be already in Hanover in my husband's pocket. I started searching in all likely and unlikely places, while the children, panic-stricken, closed their eyes and covered their ears hoping to delay the bad news that we had to turn back, pack our loosely strewn belongings into tidy suitcases, and take the train. Fortunately, I found the car paper in the glove compartment, where my husband had thoughtfully put it before departing on his trip. I let out a victory cry to be heard by the children through covered ears, and we were especially happy and cheerful during the subsequent long wait and drab border processing.

The Lost Passport: A Criminal Case

Credit for the family's most infamous lapse in safekeeping personal papers belongs to niece Susanne, who lost her West German passport together with her day visa in East Berlin. She was staying with us for a week during her summer vacation, and besides seeing four cousins from West Berlin she also wanted to visit her two cousins in East Berlin. In preparation for this excursion, my daughter, Charlotte, procured a crossing permit (*Passierschein*) and the Eastern cousins reserved a table for lunch in the *Ratskeller,* a reputable restaurant in East Berlin's city hall. At the Friedrichstrasse subway station, the two girls lined up in the proper categories: Susanne with 'citizens of the BRD (Federal Republic of Germany)' and Charlotte with 'residents of Westberlin'. They met on the other side, where the two nephews and the girlfriend of one awaited them.

Their first stop happened to be the bookstore near the station, where the girls could spend some of their mandatory exchange money, which amounted to fifty East German marks (twenty-five per person). From the store they walked along the historic boulevard *Unter den Linden* towards the *Ratskeller* on Alexanderplatz, the central square of the city. Somewhere along the way the group was shaken up by Susanne's alarm: "Where is my passport?" All pockets and handbags were searched, but no passport was found. They traced their steps back to the bookstore and to the train station, without luck. By then there was just enough time to walk to the fine restaurant and claim their reserved table. Deciding to have the pleasure first, then the pain, the group abandoned the search until after lunch. The move turned out to have been smart because Susanne thereby averted near starvation in the tribulation that followed. The *Ratskeller* reservation assured them seating ahead of those waiting in the long line at the entrance. The meal was good, and it took hardly any time to overcome the 'cultural divide' between the young people, who were growing up under two radically different systems. Charlotte served as 'glue' because she often visited the East, took along other guests from the West, and also befriended friends of her cousins. Before the Wall opened, she had already been invited to various parties and excursions by young East Berliners other than relatives.

After the meal the facts had to be faced, and everybody knew that it wouldn't be an easy matter. Experience with similar situations in the West counted for little. Charlotte and her father, for example, had once lost their papers while on a boat trip in France, forgetting the documents in a briefcase somewhere along the river. The local French police had taken this report at face value and had been more or less helpful in locating the missing briefcase. But a West German reporting a lost passport in East Berlin during the years of the Wall was treated to a criminal investigation, with the passport *loser* as the potential criminal.

The ordeal began at the entrance to the *Tränenpalast* ('Palace of Tears', the processing site for returning Westerners at Friedrichstrasse). The Easterners had to stay outside while Susanne and Charlotte entered to report the mishap to the first officer. Sure enough the girls were placed in the 'major problem' category right away (just as I had been at the same place a decade before, after having deviated from the transit route).

The two girls were taken to different frisking cabins where they had to empty their handbags and pockets. Tedious questioning started about the purpose of their visit and their contacts in the GDR. One question came up repeatedly: "To whom did you give the papers?" Susanne had to describe the layout of the first page in her passport. Because she had never traveled overseas or to Eastern Europe, she needed a passport only for an occasional visit to West Berlin. These trips were so seldom that she had never studied the document and now stammered wrong information. Her insecurity evidently encouraged the interrogator to ask several other questions that she couldn't answer correctly.

The Easterners waited outside all this time and were relieved when at least Charlotte emerged from the *Tränenpalast.* They went home together to wait for further news from Susanne. My brother-in-law felt that Susanne's father had to be informed. It took a long time to get a telephone connection to Hanover, but he finally came on the line. He fumed: "She lost her passport and the police have locked her up? It serves her right! She is not careful enough!" Later, some blame was handed down to me. The passport had slipped out of, or had been stolen from, an unzipped side pocket of an unusual, triangularly shaped shoulder bag that evidently had failed to hold its contents reliably, and I was the one who had brought this impractical object from America as a present for my niece.

The time passed very slowly for the cousins that afternoon while waiting for news of Susanne's fate. Finally, the phone rang. Susanne informed the family that she was at the Keibelstrasse police headquarters near Alexanderplatz and that she needed a person to identify her in front of the authorities. The disappearance of a passport also means the loss of one's 'personal identity'.

Susanne's predicament brought to my mind the nightmares I had had after escaping from Hungary in 1956 and again shortly before moving to West Berlin in 1977: searching for nonexistent papers at a hostile border; wanting to leave but being detained because of doubtful identity.

My niece was not as fearful as I had been, and she took the whole thing in her stride. She asked for some soap and a towel, possibly even toothpaste and a toothbrush for the uncertain duration of her captivity. Charlotte volunteered to go there and was driven by her aunt to the securely guarded huge building. She was treated as an accomplice rather than as a witness.

First came an hour to wait for no apparent reason. Then she had to identify her cousin and answer such questions as: "When and where did you first meet this person?"

Charlotte's answer was: "A long time ago when she came to visit me in my playpen. We were babies together." Then the questions about that day's visit, all answered before, were repeated several more times, the main one being:

"To whom did you give the passport?"

Finally, Charlotte had to swear that she was telling the truth. As a final act the officer on duty told her in a threatening voice: "If you have been lying to us then you will never ever be allowed to enter the German Democratic Republic again!" Slightly intimidated, but with a clear

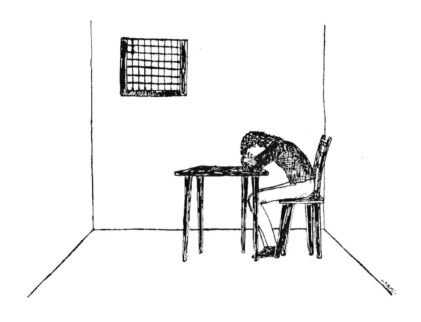

A nap without passport.

conscience, Charlotte left the building.

Susanne was lucky that she had bought books earlier on that day. She had plenty of time to read. When the routine processing of visitors returning to the West ended at midnight her case was taken up again. Fortunately, nobody had shown up at the border wanting to pass through with her documents, but neither had anyone handed them in.

To become a person again, she needed new papers. The first step in this direction was the creation of a passport photo. The machine needed for this operation at Friedrichstrasse was out of order, so two officers drove her to another location. The machine there apparently functioned, for upon returning to Friedrichstrasse, the officers attached a sleepy-looking picture of Susanne to a piece of paper containing her personal data. Several colorful stamps made it truly official, and by 2:30 a.m. she was due for release to the West.

This circumstance was not to her liking at all. The 'west area' at this train station didn't mean that one was physically in West Berlin, it just meant that one could take trains that ran to West Berlin locations. But at 2:30 a.m. no such train operated, and Susanne imagined herself waiting for three more hours on a deserted bench at the lowest level, platform D. She shuddered at the vague possibility that a few drunks still lingered there, clutching a bottle bought at the *Intershop* on that platform.

She asked the guards to take her to the Heinrich-Heine-Strasse/ Prinzenstrasse crossing instead, the checkpoint for West Germans. From there she would be able to walk until she found a taxi somewhere.

"No," said one officer. "If you enter at one crossing point, then you have to leave through the same one again."

The poor girl just didn't want to face the deserted train station alone and presented her next request: "Please take me back with you to police headquarters and let me stay there until the first train starts in the morning!" They granted her request, and at this nocturnal hour the small room with 'Swedish curtains' (meaning iron bars on the window) and locked doors seemed rather cozy compared to platform D at the Friedrichstrasse station.

Susanne did not get much sleep sitting on a chair and leaning over a table, but only two and a half hours remained anyway before two officers appeared and drove her once again to the 'Palace of Tears'. She was escorted through the control area and could finally catch a train to Lichterfelde.

Charlotte had already returned home before midnight with the sad news that her cousin was in prison. We waited up past midnight but then went to sleep. After the long vigil and without supper or breakfast, Susanne was already so confused that she got lost on the way home. Instead of the fifteen-minute walk from the Lichterfelde S-Bahn station, she wandered around much longer, arriving in time for breakfast at 8 a.m.

Weeks later her old passport arrived in the mail, but without an explanation as to where it had been found, when, and by whom. Maybe someone *had* stolen it but had not dared use it. Or perhaps the badly constructed shoulder bag had indeed been the culprit – acting as an instrument of 'capitalist (i.e., Western) sabotage'.

Mixed IDs

Just as the blood group of a donor and an acceptor have to match for a successful blood transfusion, the rules regulating the traffic through the Berlin Wall required that a 'crossee' match the crossing points. Not counting waterways and exit routes on the city's outer perimeter, there were seven checkpoints interrupting the course of the Wall between East and West Berlin. North Berliners mostly drove through the control point at Bornholmer Strasse; South Berliners, at Sonnenallee. For the Berliners traveling from the districts in-between there were Chausseestrasse and Invalidenstrasse. The Oberbaum bridge spanning the Spree river was only for Berlin pedestrians. West Germans had their exclusive crossing point at Prinzenstrasse, and they shared Bornholmer Strasse with the locals. Checkpoint Charlie was reserved for foreigners. The eighth checkpoint, the Friedrichstrasse train station, was situated not along the Wall but deep inside eastern territory, and could be used by pedestrians of all categories.

During the mid-1980s, more and more Westerners struck up contact with East Germans, either during excursions into their country or while Easterners paid visits to their West German relatives. For these East Germans it was politically safer and more neutral if they met their new Western friends at public places, like a theater or opera, rather than at their homes. As part of such a non-family friendly contact, an East Berlin couple offered to purchase opera tickets ahead of time for my colleague, J.B., and for a few of his friends. On the designated evening, the East Berlin couple appeared with ten tickets in front of the State Opera (*Staatsoper*). Eight of the ten ticket holders had to cross from West Berlin, which meant that something was likely to go wrong.

The Western organizer, J.B., and his wife, who lived in the northern district of Spandau, crossed at Bornholmer Strasse. A young colleague, T.R., took the subway to Friedrichstrasse, and I went through Checkpoint Charlie. The six of us, including the ticket carriers, had arrived at the opera in good time and waited for the missing four: a man, his wife and their two teenage children. J.B. told us that the family had moved to West Berlin from Hamburg about four years previously and had not yet been in any of the East Berlin operas or theaters. The children were seventeen and eighteen years old, and we admired these youngsters' willingness to go out with their parents to sit through the rather 'heavy' modern piece *Moses and Aaron* by Arnold Schönberg.

Or maybe not? The parents arrived without the teenagers, and the remaining two tickets could neither be sold nor given away in the short time remaining before the start of the performance. In the intermission, our attention centered on the latecomer couple as they related their adventure at the border. It turned out that the children hadn't been frightened away by Schönberg's music after all, but that the family had had to split up because the young people had not been allowed to cross into East Berlin.

According to the vivid account by the parents, the four of them had driven to the Prinzenstrasse checkpoint an hour before the performance. Four years earlier, shortly after their arrival in Berlin, they had already crossed there together on a sightseeing tour. What worked once, they thought, should work a second time because no great changes in policy had been announced since then. Still, when they handed their papers to the guard, he declared emphatically: "This crossing point is only for West Germans! The Berliners have to cross elsewhere!"

"Who are Berliners here?" they asked.

"We are all Hamburgers!"

"No," said the guard, pointing to the rather crisp new personal documents of the teenagers. "These are West Berlin IDs." He also added that, since West Berlin wasn't part of the Federal Republic of Germany, the young people couldn't claim West German citizenship, the requirement for using that particular checkpoint.

It wasn't the policy that had changed in the four years, but the status of the children. Upon their first sightseeing tour to the East, they had been thirteen and fourteen years old and had been included in the passports of the parents. When the children turned sixteen, each in turn had received personal papers at their neighborhood police station, and

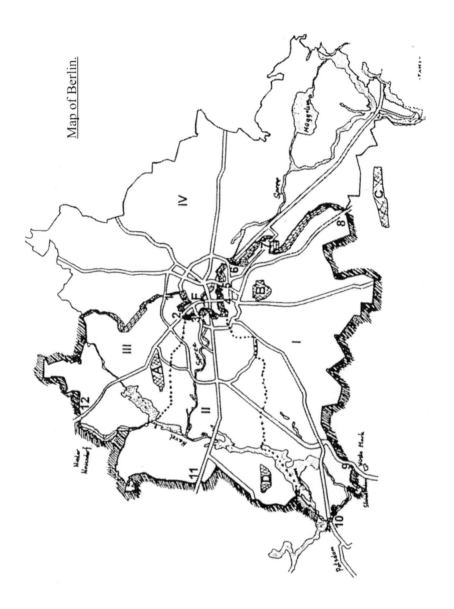

Map of Berlin.

KEY TO THE MAP OF BERLIN

Sectors of the Four Power City

West Berlin:

       I *American Sector*
     II *British Sector*
   III *French Sector*

East Berlin:

     IV *Soviet Sector*

Airports

A	*Tegel*	*West civilian and French military*
B	*Tempelhof*	*West civilian and American military*
C	*Schönefeld*	*East civilian and Soviet military*
D	*Gatow*	*British military*

Crossing Points between West and East Berlin *(for)*

F	*Friedrichstrasse train station*	*all categories*
1.	*Bornholmer Strasse*	*Berliners and West Germans*
2.	*Chausseestrasse*	*Berlin residents*
3.	*Invalidenstrasse*	*Berlin residents*
4.	*Checkpoint Charlie/ Friedrichstrasse*	*foreigners*
5.	*Prinzenstrasse/ Heinrich-Heine-Strasse*	*West Germans*
6.	*Oberbaum Bridge*	*Berlin residents (pedestrians)*
7.	*Sonnenallee*	*Berlin residents*

Crossing Points from West Berlin to the GDR *(transit to)*

8.	*Waltersdorfer Chaussee /Rudower Chaussee*	*Schönefeld Airport*
9.	*Dreilinden/Drewitz*	*West Germany*
10.	*Glienicker Bridge*	*only Allied military (spy exchange)*
11.	*Staaken*	*Hamburg and North Germany*
12.	*Heiligensee/Stolpe*	*Expressway to Hamburg*

Crossing places for railroad and ships are not marked.

that happened to have been in West Berlin. The parents had kept their West German passports, and none of them were aware of the mixed citizenship status that had thereby arisen within the family. They were stunned that the confusing facts surrounding the Four-Power status of Berlin written up in their history books – but ignored in the Free and Hanseatic city of Hamburg – had caught up with them at this checkpoint.

Not yet giving up on attending the opera performance, the parents asked where their Berliner children could cross together with them. The guard suggested Bornholmer Strasse, but before this 'mixed-up' family could have started out on their next abortive border adventure he asked: "Do the Berliners have crossing permits (*Passierscheine*)?"

The next surprise: "What is a crossing permit? Doesn't one get a visa at the border?" This response, in turn, astonished the guard, who suggested that the teenagers give up, go home, and next time gather more information, obtain a crossing permit, and go to a different check-point.

The family from Hamburg thus received a compact course in 'Berlinology'. Our amusement, which came at their expense, annoyed them. Of course, it was not the unlucky event but the ignorance of these not-so-new Berliners that sparked the laughter. One border story usually brings up another, so everybody contributed what-happened-at-the-border anecdotes. My twenty-year-old story about my husband's unsuccessful attempt to cross with the baby at Prinzenstrasse was a fitting variation on the theme of the evening, namely, mixed IDs.

The border tales had left no time to discuss anything else, so the group considered staying together longer and going to a restaurant. The logical first plan called for a restaurant in East Berlin so that our ticket-providers could come with us. Arguments against it were the long wait it might entail to get in and get served, and the Westerners had to be back at their border checkpoints before midnight. Moreover, the strictly enforced total alcohol abstinence for drivers discouraged the men, who were thirsty for a glass of beer. To make the point, J.B. recalled a firsthand account of what once happened when he didn't follow the zero-alcohol rule in the GDR. He was by no means drunk, but his trespass still cost him four hours at the Keibelstrasse police station and a DM 100 penalty. A repeat performance was to be avoided at all costs.

The next-best solution seemed to be a restaurant in West Berlin.

*A real Berlin evening: six westerners fan out to
four different checkpoints.*

Several locations were suggested, but each happened to be too far for somebody. At the moment we were indeed standing together, but to rendezvous in the West, the six Westerners in our group would first have to go to four different crossing points and then gather again on the other side. The time estimates for our respective journeys ranged between twenty and fifty minutes, with a large uncertainty factor based on the variable speed at the border stations. Finally, the obstacles won out, and we declared solidarity with the East Berliners, who couldn't have come to any of the West Berlin restaurants anyway. All plans were canceled, and the thirsty men headed to their home refrigerators by the shortest routes. For all ten of us, it had been a memorable, genuine Berlin evening with all the special trimmings that only the divided city could provide.

Backward Passports

Not all foreigners were regarded the same way by East German officials. As an American citizen, I never felt particularly welcome at the GDR border, but I found out how well I had actually been treated in comparison to real 'problem aliens' I sometimes traveled with.

My husband worked with an Israeli sociologist, Ephraim J., called Eppie, on several international comparative studies. Their cooperation started in the United States, where Eppie spent some years with his family when we lived there. Besides the scientific cooperation, a family friendship had also developed. In America our mixed nationalities had not been an issue at all, but after we moved to Berlin, that changed radically.

The initial experience was the least problematic. Upon Eppie's first visit in Berlin, we asked him what he wanted to see. He had two wishes: to see the Wall and to attend a Wagner opera. The two could be combined by going to the *Staatsoper* in East Berlin. I crossed with him at Checkpoint Charlie, while my husband went by subway through Friedrichstrasse. At the first passport check in front of the boom barrier, the border guard opened the Israeli passport, turned it around, opened it again, then turned it upside down, opened it, and became noticeably frustrated. I politely suggested that he start at the 'end' and leaf through it 'backwards'. The guard didn't like to be told what to do, but followed the suggestion and found the picture, name of the owner, and the validity date of the document. The processing was slow to normal, and we made it to the opera on time. Eppie enjoyed *Tristan und Isolde* and found it a pity that all Wagner operas were 'forbidden fruit' in his country. Of course, that made it 'sweeter' to taste somewhere else.

The next undertaking of our trio was a trip to Gothenburg, Sweden, for a project coordination meeting in 1980. The social scientists wanted to be in Gothenburg for the opening reception in the evening, so we had to leave home before 5 a.m. and catch the 10 a.m. ferry from Sassnitz in East Germany to Trelleborg, Sweden. We drove to Staaken, the only northern highway exit out of West Berlin at the time[1].

The backward passport caused some confusion at each checking stage, but the real trouble started at the East German customs inspection, where we had to park the car. With unprecedented thoroughness, or rather meanness, every little crevice of the car was checked. We even had to pry open some small plastic covers, probably place holders for absent accessories. We didn't even know that they existed, let alone how to remove or replace them. The controllers found nothing, but the waiting and frisking stole a precious hour needed to get to the ferry. The only reason we could think of for having been treated as a 'suspicious lot' was the strained Soviet-Israeli relations prevailing then. To make up the lost time while driving to Sassnitz, the drivers ignored the speed limit and risked both fines and accidents. Fortunately, it was a Sunday morning with not a soul to be seen on the bumpy roads leading through sleeping towns. The stamp in my passport testifies that we arrived at the ferry port between nine and ten in the morning.

On the way back four days later, we took a ship from Gothenburg to Travemünde in West Germany. From there we drove through the GDR on the transit highway Hamburg-Berlin, a road notorious for 'speed traps'. It had stretches where a speed limit was imposed for no apparent reason, and drivers who didn't reduce their speed instantly were stopped and fined. I sat beside the driver, watched the road signs, and called out each changed speed limit right away. Nevertheless, we were stopped by the *Volkspolizei* (People's Police) and charged with having driven 65 in a 60 km/hr zone. The violation of five km (three miles) per hour could not have lasted longer than a few seconds, for in addition to calling out the speed limit every time, I had also checked the speedometer. This charge was absurd, and probably not even true, but considering our race to Sassnitz the previous Sunday, a fine was fully deserved. Two policemen together asked for the papers of the driver and for the car registration. Eppie presented his passport and international driver's license. Again, page turning and surprises as usual.

---

[1] In 1983 another nothern transit exit opend at Heiligensee/Stolpe for the then newly build expressway to Hamburg.

'Form-filling station'.

The young policemen even admitted that they had never seen a backward passport before, so they retired to their vehicle and studied the unusual object very carefully while filling out a speeding ticket. After twenty minutes, the policemen collected the fine (ridiculously high for a three-mile-an-hour violation) and allowed us to drive on.

Of course, Israelis are not the only ones carrying passports in which the writing is 'backward' from the point of view of European languages. My personal encounter with Arabic documents occurred at Schönefeld airport around 1980. In those days, arriving passengers didn't move from the planes to the passport inspection in one steady stream, because they had to fill out a form. This caused a certain turbulence in the crowd as people picked up blank forms and searched for pens and surfaces to write on. While I was filling out my paper, a young man approached and told me in international sign language that he couldn't understand any of the languages on the form, didn't know what information was being asked for, and couldn't write Latin script. He asked for my help and trustfully handed me his passport.

My previous experience with Eppie's papers helped me recognize what kind of passport it was, so I started at the 'end' and turned the pages 'backwards'. Fortunately, all the information asked for on the form appeared in there in Latin script, not just Arabic. I copied out this data, realizing that the young man was sixteen years old and came from Sidon (Saida) in Lebanon. While I was helping him, four other young men came and lined up behind him at my 'form-filling station'. All of them were sixteen or seventeen years old, and all came from Sidon. I was curious what their destination and business was in either East or West Germany. Of course, we couldn't communicate to find out, but I had a vague feeling that it was better for me not to know. These boys were too young and too uneducated for academic studies, and it was also unlikely that this was a class excursion, or a group on a family visit. More likely they had been sent for some military commando training, but for me they were just lost children needing help in a strange environment. When fierce fighting was reported from Sidon a few years later, I thought of these youngsters, who had just grown into prime military age.

Problem Aliens

National Chinese were among the most problematic foreigners on the GDR political landscape. Whereas an Israeli passport was at least accepted as a valid identification document, a passport from Taiwan was not. I found this out the hard way at a border-control station on the Hamburg-Berlin expressway. At an international science meeting in Hamburg, I met up with my Chinese girlfriend and one-time colleague, Li-Yeh, from America. After the meeting she and her husband rented a car to tour Germany. What better way is there to embark on German sightseeing than to visit Berlin, where I had invited them to stay with me for a few days. They, in turn, offered to drive me to Berlin on the new expressway, which promised to be faster than the train ride I had planned. Late in the afternoon on August 17th, 1984, we arrived to the GDR border station at Zarrentin.

"Park the car on the side!" was the instruction after the first scan of our passports. 'Here we go again!' I thought and recalled that in the twelve years (1972-84) since 'normal' transit meant processing while staying in the car, none of my 'abnormal' processing experiences had taken less than an hour. First, we had to wait without any further instructions. Then we were told to come into the office barrack. My friends were glad that I could interpret for them because it was clear that nobody there spoke any English or Chinese, and they wouldn't have understood what the matter was with their passports. I myself could hardly believe what I heard. A Taiwanese passport was not a valid document for even a transit trip through the GDR, so both travelers had to get a 'proof of personal identity' paper (*Identitätsbescheinigung*).

"This is highway robbery!" was my quiet remark. I knew that these papers cost at least DM 20 per person, for on one occasion I also had had to get this document when the picture on my Berlin ID was 'wobbling'. Because the victims didn't have spare passport pictures with them, the procedure started in a photo booth. Then came the filling out of the forms. The officer typed very slowly with one finger, just like the one who had filled out my paper some years before. The careful spelling of the complicated Chinese names was an additional reason for a slowdown. We left the station after 9 p.m. irritated and exhausted. Usually, such a personal identity paper was only valid for one entrance and exit, so it was unclear if a repeat performance was to be expected on the trip from Berlin to Frankfurt.

The next day my guests were still interested in seeing East Berlin. I told them that I was willing to drive them anywhere in West Berlin but that they had to go without me to the East. I also explained that it would cost them a good deal of money. Even without an extra ID, they would have to exchange DM 25 per person and pay DM 5 each for a visa. This frightened them away because they had to save for the 'identity' documents they might need en route to Frankfurt am Main. In spite of their free bed and breakfast, the visit of this Chinese couple in Berlin turned out to be rather expensive. Luckily, their ID from Zarrentin was still valid on the transit expressway to Frankfurt, but in addition to the transit visa they had to pay a DM 20 fine for not wearing seat belts.

The validity of foreign papers and the permission at any one time to cross into East Berlin remained unpredictable, with hardly ever an explanation being given of why one was refused a visa. Two friends of my children, Amy from America and Pierre from France, once stayed with us at the same time. Pierre could speak German but not Amy. Since no one in our family liked to tour East Berlin with guests, we found it a great solution to send Amy and Pierre there together. They lined up at the Friedrichstrasse train station in the category *Ausländer* (foreigners) and soon advanced to the processing window. A polite Frenchman lets ladies go first, so Amy became the first of them to get a visa. She was then able to proceed to the customs and money changing area by pushing on the door in front of her when a buzzer sounded. While exchanging her currency, she already looked whether Pierre would soon be emerging from the same 'trapdoor'. No, someone else came. Then another stranger. She left the customs area with an uneasy feeling and waited outside for a whole hour. She was sad because Pierre, with the city map and his German knowledge, had deserted her. In Europe for the first time and right away alone in East Berlin, she felt lost and disoriented. While walking along aimlessly, she made sure that she didn't lose track of the return route.

Of course, poor Pierre was also having a hard time. The visa officer had not accepted his travel document as a valid French passport. Pierre was over sixteen years old but carried some youth ID that had served him well when he had traveled through the GDR by train. The ID was valid all over Europe, but not at Friedrichstrasse. His German knowledge bore no fruit when he pleaded to be let through, or at least tell Amy behind the 'trapdoor' that he couldn't follow her. Pierre came home defeated, followed shortly by Amy, whose sightseeing day had also been spoiled.

The same pattern dominated in the other direction as well. My girlfriend, Eva G., once returned from East to West Berlin with her two young sons carrying valid Hungarian passports and permanent passes (*Passierscheine*) enabling them to go back and forth between the two halves of the city. The twelve-year-old son, Kristof, was processed first and passed through the trapdoor alone, thinking that his mother and brother would follow. The officer took the other passport, issued for Eva and the younger boy, András, but did not return it. Several other travelers passed through, and Kristof started to get nervous. Every time the buzzer sounded and the door was opened by somebody, Kristof poked his head into the opening and shouted in Hungarian: "Mama come! What are you waiting for! What is the matter? Why aren't you coming?" The poor mother would have liked to know that herself, but the officer didn't say anything, just examined András and his passport photo suspiciously from time to time. When the shouting escalated and still nothing happened, Eva asked to see the superior of the processing officer. The man did come, but instead of explaining what the delay meant, he just gave an order to the subordinate officer to let the mother and child pass[1].

It was very frustrating not to get an answer, especially when one happened to be sent back from the border. The third visit of our Israeli sociologist friend, Eppie, to Berlin took place shortly after Israeli

---

[1] Eastern-bloc citizens with permanent passes did not have to get a special permit each time they crossed the border. The mother could have gone to East Berlin without her younger son, whose name was in her passport, and brought back with her another child. András was light blond and the mother had black hair. Maybe the two did not seem to fit together and thus aroused suspicion.

military forces entered southern Lebanon in June 1982. Ignoring the international crisis and my suggestion not to go to East Berlin at that time, my husband wanted to show Eppie the famous Weissensee Jewish cemetery and then visit his brother Peter. Instead of going along, I preferred to have a border-induced headache that afternoon and remarked to my husband: "I don't envy you crossing with a problem alien!"

This time Eppie took the S-Bahn to Friedrichstrasse while my husband drove by car to Invalidenstrasse. Soon he was waiting for his Israeli friend at the exit of the train station, in vain. Eppie had meanwhile presented his passport at the control window and had been told to leave the processing line and sit in a particular place. After half an hour his passport was returned to him without a visa. He asked for an explanation, but the answer was only the cold and stony remark: "Today you cannot go over!" Eppie pleaded with them to tell the professor standing at the exit door not to wait for him any longer, but the request was not even considered. Upset and angry, Eppie called me with the news.

After more than an hour's wait, my husband began trying to find out what had happened to his friend. He drove to his brother's apartment in East Berlin, for it was impossible to contact me from a telephone booth at Friedrichstrasse, not even from one equipped for long-distance dialing[1]. I tried to notify him through my brother-in-law, but I gave up after twenty-five dialing attempts. It always took extreme patience and a piece of good luck to get through. Two hours later, my husband managed to reach me from his brother's home phone and confirmed what he had already known, that his colleague had not been allowed to pass through the border that day. Ephraim never again tried to visit East Berlin until the Wall was gone and his El-Al flight from Tel Aviv landed at Schönefeld airport.

---

[1] A 'communication wall' had been erected between East and West Berlin in May 1952. At that time nearly 4000 telephone cables were physically cut between the two halves of the city, crippling intracity telephoning. Slight improvements followed in 1971 and 1978, but there were too few lines, and international rates applied for all calls. Even at great expense and with major technological effort, it took from 1990 until 1992 to construct one unified net out of the antiquated eastern system and the modern western one.

Excursions and Guided Tours

Friends and relatives who visited us in the 1970s and 1980s had one thing in common. As first priority on their sightseeing list they wanted to see the Wall. This request was easy to satisfy, since one could reach some section of it no matter which direction one went. If time was short, we went to nearby Ostpreussendamm, a street that dead-ended into the Wall. This now heavily traveled thoroughfare connecting the suburb of Lichterfelde with Seefeld and Teltow, two small communities beyond Berlin's city limits, was severed for 28 years. A large section of its pavement was broken up to make way for the Wall.

My children called the Ostpreussendamm area 'our friendly neighborhood wall' as a takeoff on some midwestern US advertisements recommending products or services in one's own suburban area. When my brother, Peter, visited us with his family from Cleveland, Ohio, the grownups and the youngsters alike were eager to see the Wall. While the parents tended to favor its historic sites like the Brandenburg Gate and Checkpoint Charlie, seven-year-old Andrew was dead set on our 'friendly neighborhood wall'. He had heard from his cousins that it was 'see-through' and that dogs were to be seen on the other side. The description was accurate. As in some other suburban locations, the Wall at Ostpreussendamm was a heavy wire mesh that allowed a glimpse into the death strip, and we once did see an armed border guard there leading a large German shepherd on a leash. The children hoped for a repeat performance.

Unfortunately, even after a long wait at the site, we couldn't offer the same spectacle for Andrew, so we told him what little we knew about these dogs. They were supposedly fierce animals trained especially to catch fugitives. It was said they could even pursue the 'enemy' in tunnels, but no 'success stories' ever leaked out. In truth, the animals had little chance to practice their skills in real life, which for them

Nostalgic 'Wall dog'.

consisted of being led on a leash by stone-faced officers, who had to avoid personal friendship with these dogs, so that their character would not be 'softened'.

When the Wall came down, more than five thousand Wall dogs lost their jobs. In the ensuing discussion of whether they should be shot or sold, the population came out for the latter solution, and the dogs became media stars. Indeed, many of the potential new owners expected to find well-trained, aggressive dogs to protect their houses and gardens. To general surprise, the dogs were not fierce but fearful. These brainwashed creatures had been trained not to bark and had spent most of their lives on a leash between high walls. Owners reported that their new charges played with neither people nor other dogs. They turned out to be withdrawn and timid. In search of a place that resembled their previous home setting, they tended to settle near stone walls, where they could sit still for hours. The happy end is that most of the wall-dogs could be deprogrammed. After six months of love, care and patience, they played, barked, cuddled, and lived the life of normal, friendly household animals.

Other relatives of ours had other special 'favorite' sites. During his 1978 visit, my father took a sightseeing bus tour and, wanting to take pictures, asked me afterwards to take him again to "that particular place where the Wall looked especially depressing". Since I found the Wall very depressing at most places, I had to ask for more specific information. "The place where they have lookout platforms for tourists, some souvenir shops, and fast food stands." I suggested Checkpoint Charlie and the Brandenburg Gate, but he insisted that the particular site in question was so much more gruesome than those main tourist attractions. Then he mentioned walled-in windows and a church in the no-man's-land. So off we went to Bernauer Strasse, an unlucky place where the border ran along the entire length of the street separating the West Berlin district of Wedding to the north from the East Berlin district of Mitte (Center) to the south.

Strictly respecting the territorial rights of the Western Allies in the divided city, the builder of the Wall had kept exactly to the given demarcations. In this case, the land register showed that the line between East and West coincided exactly with the façades of the houses on the south side of the street. As one inhabitant later described it: "When we leaned out the windows, our heads were in the West and our backsides were in the East." Closing the border therefore meant walling up the front entrance doors. As soon as the inhabitants were commanded to move out of their apartments through the back door, one person after another climbed out the front windows, descending on sheets they had tied together or jumping onto safety nets provided by the West Berlin fire department.

When my father went there in 1978, several houses on the south side had been already torn down and the doors and windows of the remaining façades securely walled up. The Church of Reconciliation (*Versöhnungskirche*), which was the Lutheran church of the Bernauer Street parish community, stood empty, orphaned, and inaccessible from either side. It offered a sorry sight in the middle of the particularly strong fortifications on this border strip. This church had an unhappy end, for after razing the last of the walled-up houses and façades, the East German authorities blew it up in 1985. When the houses and the forlorn church had disappeared, the 'especially gruesome' look changed to an 'ordinary wall-landscape'. My father did not live to see it. A Wall memorial park is now set up on the large empty space left by the missing row of houses and a new chapel replaced the Church of Reconciliation.

My mother's 'favorite place' happened to be the small south-western community of Steinstücken. This conglomeration of two dozen houses was clearly outside city limits, but still belonged to Berlin. After some negotiation East Germany 'generously' permitted use of the connecting road, so the wall came to flank it on both sides and encircled the cluster of houses. At the time of the Wall, this road was probably the most brightly lit street in the world, but not for the sake of the vehicles driving on it. The lamps were installed to maintain daylight conditions on the death strip at all times. The omnipresence of the Wall gave the village of Steinstücken a special quality that provided the 'ultimate Wall experience' for my mother. In the winter of 1989-90 she suggested we go there to see the changes. Although most of the wall along the road remained in place, several sections were already missing around the houses, revealing to the inhabitants the surrounding meadows and forests.

I was confronted by my most depressing section of the Wall every time I took the S1, a north-bound S-Bahn line. It traveled a stretch of several kilometers where the border happened to run along the tracks.

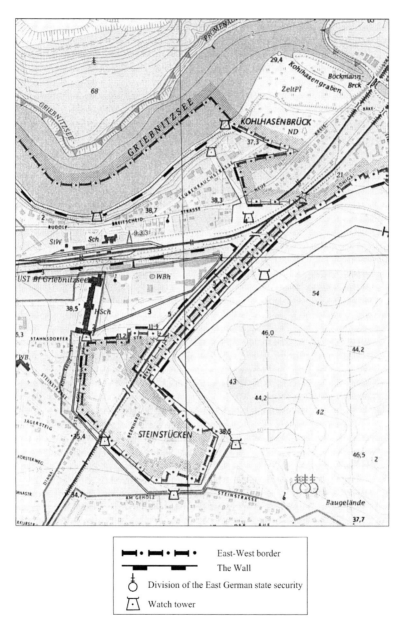

▮━•▮━•▮━•	East-West border
▬▬▬▬▬	The Wall
⊥⊙	Division of the East German state security
⧉	Watch tower

Exact military map of Steinstücken from GDR archives.

121

The houses to the right and left of the tracks stood surprisingly close to each other. In the early days of the Wall, when West Berliners could not obtain passes to visit their relatives in the East, 'waving dates' were arranged by renting windows facing each other across the tracks. In this setting Grandma could be given at least some view of her new grandchild, or a lonely mother could glimpse her beloved son with his new wife. Since the lines S1 and S3 were part of the West Berlin public transportation system, East Berliners had to be prevented at all costs from gaining access to these tracks or to trains using them. The fortifications looked correspondingly cruel. The houses on the East side seemed drab compared to those on the West side, and the ugly ghost stations topped off the impression of collective misery. I could never get used to this sight, and it upset me every time I saw it.

Still, my most memorable Wall shock hit me during an outing that I didn't even expect to take me near the border. The university's science institute where I work had chartered a boat for its annual staff excursion. Berlin has more waterways, rivers and canals than Venice, and one can crisscross the city on the water, passing residential, historical, and industrial areas. We boarded the ship in Neukölln and traveled for several hours along a series of canals, eventually turning north into the Havel river, which widens into several lakes. Our destination was the resort-like suburb of Heiligensee.

For most of the trip, we all sat or stood outside in the balmy weather, eating, drinking, conversing, and watching the landscape. The suburb of Spandau, whose inhabitants like to think of it as an independent city, floated by on our left and was followed by the dense, green Spandau Forest. On the right the last of the small communities before Heiligensee, Konradshöhe, was to be seen. I did not consult a map and just assumed that Spandau, the largest district in the British Sector[1], stretched further north and would stay with us on the left until we landed on the right-hand shore. Wrong assumption, faulty geography. Unexpectedly, the Wall 'came out' of the forest at right angles to the waterway and continued north, closely following the shoreline. The forest continued behind the Wall for a while but then ended. Nothing was to be seen, just a few meters of pure sand and the Wall with its characteristic tubular top. Soon a watchtower indicated that this area

[1] Site of the famous prison that for decades housed only one prisoner, the Nazi war criminal Rudolf Hess, who was serving a life sentence. He died in 1987.

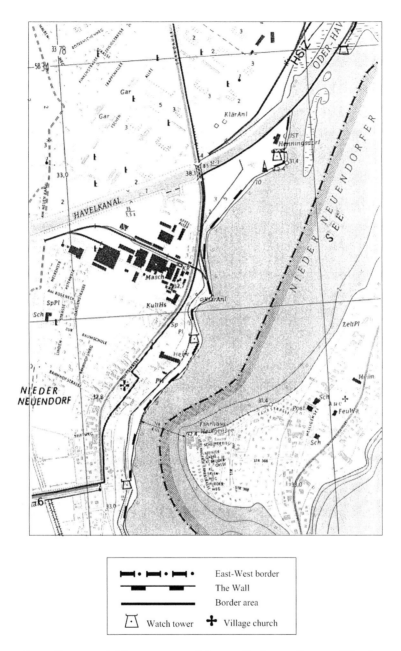

East German Military map of the walled-in village of Nieder Neuendorf. East Germans could only enter the 'border area' with special permits, and Westerners not at all. The East–West border runs through the middle of the lake.

was heavily guarded.

While observing the bathers and boaters on the West Berlin side, I wondered if anybody lived behind the wall and if they would have liked to cool off in the water but could not get to it. The answer came in the form of a church spire. It was not a fancy big tower, just the top half of the steeple of a village church standing behind the wall and peeking over it. It seemed like an outstretched arm, an SOS signal sent up from a small community calling to the outside world: "Please help us, we are walled in!" This sad appeal moved me, and tears started rolling down my cheeks. I turned so that my colleagues shouldn't see that I was crying. There were so many other waterfront wall stretches to be seen around West Berlin that the 'seasoned natives' hardly gave this one a second look. Maybe I overreacted, but since I had never gotten used to the Wall, I was still susceptible to 'Wall shocks'.

Ten years after that excursion and five years after the opening of the Wall, I visited this village, called Nieder Neuendorf (meaning Lower New Village). It is certainly not a tourist attraction, in spite of its long waterfront. The main street runs parallel to the river, and the houses on its river side are, in 1995, still in worse shape than those on the other. I conversed with some of the inhabitants and elicited some interesting information. The river side of the road had been considered 'border area' (*Grenzgebiet*), a territory that could only be entered by those living there. Locals wanting to visit these inhabitants had to get special permits to do so. Their western relatives had been categorically denied such permits. Some house owners had sold their unattractive 'wall-front' lots very cheaply to move away from the border area and are now envious of the buyers who own these valuable waterfront lots.

Where once a virginal sand beach lay outside the Wall, the water's edge is now a thicket of reeds, large shrubs, and tall weeds. It is hard to believe that this jungle spontaneously seeded itself in five years, but it is true. My informant told me that both the beach outside the Wall and the area between the two strands indeed had been pure sand when they first became accessible in 1989. The remnants of the 'patrol road', which indicate what was once the middle of the death strip, is used now by bicyclists and bathers. A dilapidated watchtower[1] still stands near the

---

[1] The administration of the nearby town of Henningsdorf renovated the tower and opened a 'border museum' in it in 2001.

south end of the village. All the windows are broken and graffiti cover its sides. At this site enough jungle has been cleared away to allow bathers access to the water for a swim. I have already gone there armed with towel and bathing suit to defy the memory of the Wall by going swimming once in Nieder Neuendorf.

"What Are You Doing All the Time in Eastern-bloc Countries?"

Mistrust on the political scene was one of the most typical characteristics of the Cold War. Who mistrusted whom? To simplify the analysis, one could say that almost everybody mistrusted everybody else. The 'other side', considered to be the enemy, was especially suspicious, but the authorities of all countries were wary even of their own citizens if they seemed to associate with the 'other side'. In few places did this rule of life seem more apparent than in West Berlin, sometimes called the 'spy capital of the world'. The reason was the city's location. A riddle circulating in those years fittingly characterized it: 'At the North Pole the only direction is south. At the South Pole all directions are north. Where is the only point on the globe where every direction is east?' The answer was 'West Berlin'. Indeed, no matter which direction one took to leave the city, one wound up in, or over, East Germany. This fact made its mark – or rather, many marks – on my passport.

Every trip through the GDR resulted in the addition of at least two colorful stamps. Recently, an expert explained to me the secrets of these stampings. The greatest one was that the ink used for the stamping also contained invisible, fluorescent components that could be seen only under ultraviolet light. That was why one's papers always disappeared under the sill of the processing window. The stamps were being examined under fluorescent light. At irregular intervals changes were made in both the visible and invisible colors. This regimen had to be kept up because the suspect citizenry of the GDR never ceased plotting its escape – if not by building clever land, water, or air contraptions, then by forging documents. Before receiving an exit stamp, the traveler always had to wait for the validity of the entrance

The location of West Berlin: '. . . Every direction is east!'

stamp to be examined. The ink pad had two visible colors. One of them was for the upper half, which contained the coat of arms, the letters *DDR* (for German Democratic Republic), the picture of a vehicle, the date, and the time of the day. The other color was used for the lower part, which bore the name of the crossing point and the number identifying the control officer. I don't know how many officers there were, but the numbers in my passport range from a '001' in Sassnitz to a '100' at Drewitz, both from 1986.

The facts immortalized in these rubber stamps were framed by an intricate design, making the stamps even more difficult to forge. I used to admire the small pictures in the upper right corner, where the vehicle of locomotion was illustrated. For every flight out of Schönefeld, one got a little airplane; for the ferry at Sassnitz (to and from Sweden), a ship with two funnels (or radar towers?); for the highway entering and exiting the control point at Drewitz, a car in front of a truck, and for various train rides out of West Berlin a badly resolved blob that must have been an electric train. No bicycles or motorcycles were allowed to tour inside the GDR – perhaps only for lack of a fitting picture on these stamps.

All socialist countries liked to decorate passports, and because I traveled quite a lot both to the West and the East, my 'stamp collection' grew rapidly. Each visitor's visa to a socialist country filled a whole page; so did each transit visa (except in the GDR). I was in Warsaw, Poland, for a scientific conference and several times in Hungary to visit relatives. Furthermore, the cheapest and shortest train connection to my daughter in Vienna, Austria, led me through Czechoslovakia. And so it went. The problem was that a standard US passport has twenty-four pages, eighteen of which are for visas. A single page could hold no more than eight GDR transit stamps, or one visitor's visa from an Eastern-bloc country. In addition the West Berlin residence permit (*Aufenthaltserlaubnis*) resided also on a full page. Hence, my 1980-1985 US passport was full before it had expired. After explaining this matter at the US consulate in Berlin in preparation for my next trip, I received an accordion extension of twelve pages glued on to the last visa page. The clerk at the counter made it official, and I was fixed up for many more colorful GDR transit stamps (and experiences).

In February 1985 I had planned a skiing trip in Austria and had booked a berth in a sleeping compartment on a train to Munich. On the

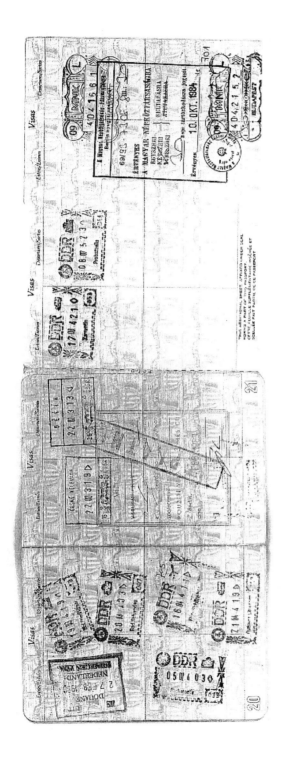

Accordion extension to US passport. The stamp collection shows transit crossings through the GDR by train three times, by airplane once, and by automobile twice, en route to Vienna through the CSSR on February 22nd, 1983, and a visit to Hungary in 1984.

evening of departure my younger daughter was admiring my odd accordion passport when she announced her discovery: "Your passport expires in three days!" I became panicky. Would I have to cancel the skiing trip, or could I just pretend I hadn't noticed anything? On the way back, when the passport will have expired, the document would be checked upon leaving Austria, and again upon entering West Germany. The East Germans, as always, would check me both at entry and exit. The chances of getting through four different inspections without the passport's expiration being detected were virtually nil.

The best solution seemed to be to sacrifice just one day of skiing, not the whole week. I had to leave the mountain and travel to Salzburg in the hope that picture-taking, developing, passport application, and completion could all be managed in one working day. A picture from a photo machine would certainly not do for a US passport. Back then it had to be a black and white, 2 by 2 inches (5 x 5 cm), 'moon-faced' exposure, that is, a full front view (without a hat or dark glasses) showing at least part of both ears. Most important of all, the background had to be white. I have seen passport pictures rejected because the background was only a hazy gray. This experience worried me when I examined my picture, which, fortunately, could be picked up on the same day it was taken.

In the early afternoon of February 11th, I arrived at the American Consulate in Salzburg with my old passport, new pictures, and a nervously beating heart. A throng of American citizens milled around in the hallways and I got apprehensive. 'Everybody is waiting for a new passport!' I thought. Fortunately this wasn't the case. The crowd was waiting to see one of the tax advisors, who make a yearly visit to all US embassies and consulates around the world to help 'Uncle Sam's children' fill out their incomprehensible tax forms. Since I had come on different business, I was soon eye to eye with the American consul. What started as a friendly conversation turned into a serious hearing. The consul looked at my old passport, pulled out the accordion extension, and counted or estimated the collection of stamps. Then with quite some suspicion in his voice, he asked, "What are you doing all the time in Eastern-bloc countries?" I felt like a black sheep, the potential spy, the accused criminal, and had to defend myself. I explained that fate landed me in West Berlin, and no matter where I went, except on flights from Tegel airport to the West, my passport was

"What Are You Doing All the Time
in Eastern-bloc Countries?"

stamped. He probed further: "You never travel to the United States?"

My reply: "Of course I do, I was there last summer!" He browsed among the many stamps, but couldn't find the simple notation reading 'US Immigration' dated 1984. He was simply assuming that everybody's passport was routinely stamped on arrival. Unfortunately, I couldn't remember what had happened in the turbulently crowded hall after landing at Kennedy Airport in New York, so my credibility was again at stake. Eventually my interrogator relented, completed the procedure, and handed me a new US passport – this one valid even for ten years, from 1985 to 1995. Since that visit in Salzburg, I am now more alert and watch to see if the US immigration official takes only a fleeting glance at my passport or documents my landing for posterity with a stamp. Once, I asked one of these people: "Don't you stamp my passport?" The officer, who held me to be an over-eager stamp collector, answered with a smile: "Not today lady, next time!" So much for the exact documentation of my landings in the United States!

The visa pages of my new passport filled up just as quickly as ever, and in the summer of 1989 the next 'accordion extension' seemed inevitable. Page eighteen was exhausted with a host of stamps, including two brown and blue ones from Schönefeld airport and one from Helsinki airport. The dates provided clear evidence that I had flown from Schönefeld to Helsinki and had come back a few days later, on July 24th, 1989. Upon re-entering the GDR, I didn't realize what a historic moment was passing as Schönefeld agent '018', whoever that was, stamped my passport. If I had known that I wouldn't need any additional pages for future transit stamps, because this was the very last 'DDR' marking ever to be put into my passport, then I would have been moved to tears and would have embraced '018' to say farewell to him and to an era.

Thaw: *"Herr Professor, Where Is Your Violin?"*

An amazing aspect of the processing at the border was the centrally directed 'collective character' of the controllers. One didn't have to read political analyses in newspapers to find out the state of the cold war between the two Germanys, one just had to listen to the first greeting or grunting of the control officer at one of the crossing points. Conversely, if the newspapers reported political storm, then it was better to skip a planned pleasure trip to East Berlin or to Potsdam. I once overheard a woman bitterly complaining to her friend about how long and tedious her crossing to East Berlin had been the day before, a lament to which the friend replied matter-of-factly: "You should know by now that you don't go to East Berlin on the day when the West German Chancellor is showing the Wall to the American President."

Although the command to shoot fugitives who tried to overcome the border fortifications remained in effect, by the mid-1980s the GDR was making a certain effort to project a more normal and benign image to the world. This included permits for East Germans to attend family events other than funerals of next of kin. If an aunt or uncle in the West turned 80 or 85, then not only retirees, but younger relatives too, could attend the celebrations. A silver anniversary of a brother or sister was also sufficient reason for issuing a visiting permit.

Another conscious effort to polish the country's image included the attempt at more civilized communication at the control points. This wasn't easy, because old habits die hard. If western travelers were tense, grimly expecting unfriendly treatment, then it was likely that the guards quickly found their way back into their 'usual style' of using a harsh voice and showing a stony face. But one well-documented incident initiated a perceptible change. A middle-aged West German traveler with a medical heart condition was interrogated about some

Where is your violin?

irregularity in his transit behavior, at which event he died. His corpse arrived home with a large open wound on the head, and newspaper headlines speculated whether he had been hit with a hammer or tortured with another object. Later explanations made it plausible that he had collapsed with a heart attack and had fallen onto a cast iron radiator. The media also reported other, similar occurrences where people had suffered heart attacks or strokes because of the stressful atmosphere at the border. The GDR took this threat to its image seriously and promised to try to avoid such incidents.

Whether centrally directed, or voluntary, the changes at the border did indeed make it less exhausting for us to be checked as human beings by 'people' rather than processed like objects by ill-tempered 'machines'. This noticeable improvement reduced the subjective obstacles separating us from our relatives in East Berlin. It also happened around this time that my brother-in-law purchased a new piano and my husband an old violin, so the brothers were motivated to play together more often than in the years before. My husband usually applied for a multiple visa, valid for three months. The owner of this valuable card only had to go once to the *Passierscheinstelle* (crossing-permit office) to get a day pass for a particular visit.

My husband sought out the less crowded hours at the nearest *Passierschein* office and went there with his violin. After receiving his pass, he drove to Invalidenstrasse on the way to brother Peter's home in East Berlin. There was a certain regularity to these visits, and the violin was written up every time as 'an object of value' (*Wertgegenstand*) when carried in, so that it would be allowed to be carried out again. On a sunny spring afternoon, a walk around a nearby lake instead of the usual sonata rehearsal was planned, and my husband didn't take his violin along. He showed his papers, exchanged the compulsory DM 25 and proceeded to customs. Upon opening the trunk and showing a shopping bag with coffee and fruit as presents, the officer took a closer, searching look into the car. This curious extra look wasn't unusual, but then came the most unusual and totally unexpected question: "*Herr Professor,* where is your violin?" Being addressed with a title showed respect, and the friendly question sounded like a sociable inquiry directed towards regular customers in a neighborhood store. My husband acknowledged it with an amiable explanation, and for days he raved about this extra-ordinary experience.

The violin-piano duo at my brother-in-law's house was sometimes fortified by my daughter Gabriella, making a trio. The afternoon of New Year's Eve 1986/87 was planned to be such an occasion, with my mother and I joining in as listeners. Our party had to divide up according to nationalities: my husband and daughter as Berlin residents, and my mother and I as foreigners. The perennial question of who should take the car was decided by seniority, entitling my seventy-eight-year-old mother to a ride. I became the driver, and Checkpoint Charlie became the crossing point. The Berlin residents who had obtained the proper passes rode the S-Bahn to the Friedrichstrasse control point. My husband took his violin along, but my daughter deposited her bulky cello in my car, reminding me to have it registered at the border for the trip back. After twenty-five years of encounter with the Wall, it turned out that we still didn't know all the crossing rules and had to learn new ones.

The cello did make me apprehensive, and I mentioned it to the first visa-handling officer at Checkpoint Charlie. "Do you want to play your cello on the street?" he asked. "No, at my brother-in-law's house." I didn't complicate matters with the explanation that the instrument wasn't even mine, but I did mention that my husband was on his way with a violin and that it was always written up at the crossing. Then came the revelation that West Berliners may take valuables into the GDR, but foreigners may not.

Surprised and unhappy I sadly awaited the next decision about whether they would want to guard the cello at the station until my return or send me back home to get rid of it. None of these. The officer asked if I had planned to return before midnight. I said yes. He acknowledged this answer, handed me a visa, and sent me to the compulsory exchange window. 'And the cello?' was on the tip of my tongue, but somehow he implied that there was nothing more to discuss. I returned to the car with the exchange money, and the customs officer waved me to the next checking station. Through non-verbal communication, I was made to understand that there wasn't a cello there, only the declared presents of oranges and brandy. The customs agent rattled down the usual record: "Do you carry firearms, explosives, books, or magazines?"

"No, none of those." He took a blank look into the trunk where the 'transparent' cello was resting in its case. He didn't mention it, I didn't mention it, and I was allowed to drive on.

The evening was pleasant with much food and music. As the driver of a car in the GDR, I strictly adhered to the rule not to touch any alcohol but glanced at my watch frequently and suggested an early return. My mother and I drove to the crossing point, where we had to get out of the car and open the trunk and the hood to expose all the possible hiding places for stowaways. I showed my papers, opened the trunk, and worried quietly, but kept my part of the non-verbal agreement (as I understood it) that if I didn't mention the cello, then it wasn't there. The second act of this pantomime went just as well as the first, and nothing unusual was found. Back in the car again and on the way out, I smiled at somebody, standing in a doorway, who seemed to be the mastermind of this pantomime. It was out of the question to thank him because the 'agreement' didn't state that I was allowed to take the instrument. We just pretended that there was no instrument, so no favor had been done. The 'mastermind' looked around, making sure that nobody was watching him directly, and returned an ever so slight, conspiring smile.

The Last Roar of the Toothless Lion:
A Souvenir Visa

Two mental games were often played by our Wall-conscious visitors. The first one, practiced mostly by mechanically talented people, involved observing the fortifications of the Berlin Wall and thinking up innumerable methods, none of them tried out, for sneaking through either the controls or the physical barriers. While showing their western passports at a crossing point, the eyes of these visitors scanned the surroundings for loopholes where somebody less fortunate than they (i.e., someone without the necessary papers) could slip through.

The other 'game' was initiated by socially and politically alert people. It consisted of contemplating the opening of the Wall. One such friend, R.G., whose hobby is still to survey opinions and ask many strange questions, had already started to take bets in 1961 as to the duration of the Wall. On a visit to Berlin twenty-two years later, he rode with me to the *Glienicke Brücke,* the bridge that connects Berlin to Potsdam. This bridge wasn't open for East-West crossing traffic, but neither was it walled up like the Brandenburg Gate. Allied military vehicles could drive across it. This semi-permeable barrier, which had come to fame through some historical spy exchanges, was guarded on one side by West Berlin policemen and on the other by East German border guards and Soviet soldiers.

On the occasion of our walk to this southwestern edge of the city, my inquisitive friend asked the policeman standing at the bridge: "What do you think, how long will this bridge still have to be guarded?" The policeman answered with a shrug of his shoulder and wasn't willing to go into a conversation with a nut who asked such provocative questions. At our dinner table five years later, the same friend asked his pet question again: "What do you think, how long will the Wall still stand in Berlin?" Half of the dozen people present were already born into the walled-in situation and a further two were small children in 1961, but we were all more communicative than the policeman at the Glienicke bridge. Everybody agreed that the existence of the Wall was so unnatural that it could not stand 'forever', but nobody foresaw imminent change. The estimates ranged from seven years to fifty. My problem with this topic was always that I couldn't imagine the Wall would disappear without violence, so I couldn't look forward to it and wished for it to happen without my presence.

Future historians, political scientists, and economists will be explaining the opening of the Berlin Wall and its complete dismantling by July 1st, 1990, as an inevitable, logical consequence of the events prior to November 1989. But had they sat at our dinner table in 1988, none of them would have predicted that in less than two years the last stretches of the Wall would be carried away or ground up and used to rebuild roads that it had cut off almost three decades before.

The rapid changes that took place in 1989-90 seemed like miracles at the time, which shows how much people had gotten used to the status quo. Of course, the Wall didn't disappear overnight on November 9th, 1989, when thousands of East Berliners streamed into the West. It is said that a controlled passage for East Germans with proper paperwork was intended but that the huge crowds assembling at the crossing points, minutes after the radio announced this new possibility, couldn't be kept back. The gates were opened to avoid a violent confrontation. This version is all the more believable because, indeed, after the first few days of freely streaming crowds, 'order' was re-established. Everybody had to show the proper papers. The Easterners had to obtain crossing permits, and the Westerners still had to exchange the usual DM 25 into East Marks. The border guards didn't become unemployed. In fact, more of them were needed because so many new crossing points opened.

To cut through the two-meter-thick wall at the Brandenburg Gate took until December 22nd, 1989. Because this historic opening drew huge crowds, it became a second free-for-all without paperwork. On that day my daughter, Gabriella, had just landed at Tegel airport for the Christmas holidays, and my mother and I went to meet her. On the way home we listened to the car radio and heard the speeches broadcast live from the opening ceremony. Both my eighty-one-year-old mother and my twenty-year-old daughter pressured me to drive as close as possible to the Gate, park, and walk through, which we did. My mother had passed through the Brandenburg Gate before, the last time being in 1932, prior to the birth of almost everyone in that dense crowd in 1989.

A few days later it was also 'business as usual' at this special crossing point as far as paperwork was concerned. With colleagues from Berlin and from Budapest, I did not pass through because one person in our party had forgotten to carry her ID, and Hungarian citizens could go through only at the controls designated for foreigners. In March 1990, three months after the abolishment of the compulsory exchange for West Germans and West Berliners, I paid my last problematic visit to Checkpoint Charlie, which was still functioning more or less the way I had known it for twenty-seven years. Riding in a Hungarian car, a Hungarian, a Pole, and I were on our way to a seminar at the Academy of Sciences in Adlershof in East Berlin to which members of our institute at the Free University had been invited by East Berlin colleagues. They had visited us in Dahlem shortly after the Wall had opened, but a return visit made sense only if there was no longer a requirement to exchange DM 25 per person.

In addition to my American passport, I carried a West Berlin ID, which made it possible to cross as a West Berliner. When we pulled into Checkpoint Charlie, I showed this ID and claimed that the new regulation allowed me to pass without a visa or a mandatory exchange. The guard, however, explained that it was still 'business as usual' at Checkpoint Charlie. In other words, West Berliners weren't allowed to pass, and every western foreigner had to pay a DM 5 visa fee and exchange DM 25. He added that I could pass free of charge with my West Berlin ID at another crossing point (and miss the lecture at Adlershof). The Hungarian and Polish passengers weren't required to exchange western money or pay for their visas, but I was still the rich capitalist and had to spare DM 30 for a ride through this exclusive checkpoint. I argued further that I would leave East Berlin by subway through Friedrichstrasse anyway because my Hungarian friend had further business in East Berlin. This had, of course, been impossible in earlier times because the visa, called a counting card (*Zählkarte*) in eastern border-jargon, permitted one to leave again only on the same

02008   EL 5542293

Deutsche Demokratische Republik

DDR

Anlage zum Paß

Nr.

VISUM

zur einmaligen Einreise für einen Tagesaufenthalt in der Hauptstadt der Deutschen Demokratischen Republik, Berlin, und Ausreise bis 24.00 Uhr des Ausstellungstages über die gleiche Grenzübergangsstelle der DDR zu Berlin (West)

A 101

Hauptstadt der DDR
Berlin

Mit dem Visum darf das Stadtgebiet der Hauptstadt der DDR nicht verlassen werden. Die S-Bahn kann nur bis zu den angegebenen Bahnhöfen benutzt werden.

The front side of the 'souvenir visa' is stamped March 22nd, 1990. The reverse side shows the S-Bahn stations within East Berlin that were permitted destinations for the holder of the visa. (Most train lines did not end within city limits.)

141

day and at the same place as it was issued. But how could such a regulation be enforced while the system was disintegrating and heads were counted at one place but not at others?

The border official listened to my return plans with a disapproving expression and commanded with his most authoritarian voice:

"You *have* to return here!"

'You can't make me do it!' was on my mind, but I only murmured "Hm" to shorten the procedure. Of course, I returned at Friedrich-strasse by waving my Berlin ID and kept the visa as a souvenir. I still had some misgivings about having been counted as entering East Berlin, but not as ever having left, so for the rest of its existence I carefully avoided Checkpoint Charlie.

My sigh of relief was deep when I watched on television as a crane lifted away the last remnants of this location of so much nuisance.

Two Reports from December 1989

November 9th, 1989

December 9th, 1989

Dear Friends,

You have all read in the paper and watched on TV the opening of the Berlin Wall, so I don't want to describe the euphoric crowd that alternately danced and hammered away on it. I just want to give a short report on how our family lived through these exciting days.

Geographic distribution of the family on November 9th: Father Burk as usual at the university during the day and at home by 6 p.m. Charlotte, who usually lives in the Kreuzberg area of Berlin, 'Daddy-sitting' at our home, because mother Marianna is away at a scientific meeting in Seattle, Washington. Gabriella at her music school near Essen, in West Germany, about a six-hour drive from Berlin.

In the 7 p.m. news Burk hears that 'soon' (day not specified) every East German will be able to get a permit to travel to West Berlin and West Germany. Quick-thinking Burk figures that 'soon' impenetrable crowds will fill the crossing points between East and West Berlin and that the last possible time to visit brother Peter in East Berlin is now. Immediately, he takes the subway (S-Bahn) to Friedrichstrasse, one of the pedestrian crossing points to East Berlin. The guards are unusually easygoing and 'forget' to demand the usual DM 25 ($14) exchange into East Marks.

The mood in the East Berlin family is especially light-hearted, and Burk parts with the words: "Next time I'll see you all at my house in Lichterfelde." The two young nephews, Peter (28) and Ludwig (26), born and raised in East Berlin, haven't seen the other half of their native city to this day (November 9th). Burk returns home before 11 p.m. without noticing much at the underground labyrinth of the Friedrichstrasse crossing point.

Charlotte watches the reports on TV as various crossing points open up. She and a girlfriend set out to see the spectacle in person. First they go to Prinzenstrasse (until now a crossing point only for West Germans) and then to the livelier Checkpoint Charlie (until now the crossing point only for foreigners). There the celebration is already in full swing, with champagne corks popping everywhere, while a bumper-to-bumper column of Trabants (small East German cars) and happy pedestrians cross the border. Some of the West spectators walk over to the East, this time free of charge and without a visa. Somebody leads around a bear on a leash, the animal on the coat-of-arms of Berlin, and the carnival atmosphere is complete. Although it is 2 a.m. by now, small children, from both East and West, are in the crowd on this crazy night.

Charlotte meets some other friends and joins them for a look at the Brandenburg Gate. This isn't a gate that can easily be opened because a two-meter-thick concrete wall is in front of it. The only way to conquer this obstacle is to climb on it and over it. When Charlotte arrives, hundreds of people are already on the Wall. Her Australian companion joins them in seconds, pulled up by others already on the wall. Charlotte finds the climb physically and psychologically too formidable. The wall is high and nobody promises that the sacrilege of trespassing on this 'holy' protector of communist suppression won't be punished by a round of machine-gun fire. She mingles in the crowd and waits until the others return from a short walk on the other side.

Charlotte is sure that her girlfriend, Cati, from East Berlin is already in the West somewhere and goes around to the houses of their mutual friends and the pubs near their houses. Finally, she and Cati find each other and have breakfast together. By this time it is 8 a.m. and Charlotte has to call at her job to take the day off.

Gabriella returns home to her little apartment near Essen, late on the evening of the 9th, after a concert and a subsequent stop in a pizza restaurant. Her telephone is ringing when she enters. Isabel, her friend and piano partner from Berlin, is calling to tell her the sensational news. Gabi has firm plans to spend the weekend practicing a lot and goes to sleep. By next morning the news 'sinks in', and she gets very excited. She is sure that she has to be where the action is. Lacking the money for

145

a train ticket and the time to go to the bank before the next train leaves for Berlin, she finds some other 'wall tourists' through a ride-coordination agency and leaves for Berlin by car in the afternoon.

The otherwise grim border crossing at Helmstedt is the scene of a joyous celebration. Everybody who isn't driving is drinking champagne. An endless row of 'Trabbis' is going to the West, and a comparable crowd of 'wall tourists' is heading for Berlin. Gabriella arrives home in Lichterfelde after midnight. It is Saturday morning, and the weekend is just beginning.

Marianna finally manages to get through on the telephone Saturday morning Pacific time and Saturday evening Berlin time. Just as one couldn't get through to San Francisco after the earthquake (on October 17th, 1989), the Berlin telephone net is now overloaded by the great event. Friends who haven't been in touch for years call from the United States, England, and Australia just to say how excited and happy they are. Marianna's first question: "What is the head count of overnight dwellers?" On Thursday it was two, by Saturday it has jumped to eight. There are two new arrivals from East Berlin and two from Leipzig. The East Berliners are Charlotte's friends; the Leipzigers, the relatives of our tenant, G., who had defected from the East in April. Our relatives from East Berlin follow Burk's recent invitation and also come to visit over the weekend, but they live so close that they don't stay overnight.

Marianna returns to Berlin on the 21st of November. She has, of course, followed the developments on TV and in the papers but has no idea how much of the Wall is still standing. If others are also wondering, here is the present picture (December 9th, 1989).

The Wall is still up, except that several new crossing points have been cut into it. At these places East Germans may enter West Berlin if they have an exit visa, and West Berliners may enter East Berlin if they have an entry visa and exchange DM 25 to East Marks one-to-one. The 'free for all' of the first day lasted only over the weekend of November 11-12th, but it is announced (on December 6th) that no visa and no exchange will be required for West Germans and West Berliners after January 1st. This regulation might go into effect sooner for the Christmas holidays.

On December 3rd, the Sunday family coffee hours in Lichterfelde resumed after twenty-eight years. These family gatherings had been started by Burk's grandmother after Burk's parents moved to West

Berlin in 1953. Sister Sabine and brother Peter attended regularly; the other brother, Ulrich, and Burk himself came only during school vacations. In August 1961, the Wall cut Peter and his wife off from these gatherings. Peter's first visit to West Berlin after 1961 was for his father's funeral (1965); the second one, for his mother's funeral (1970). Lately, there have been a few other opportunities, like sister Sabine's sixtieth birthday and our silver wedding anniversary. These visits required lots of red tape. For instance, one had to send a notarized copy of the twenty-five-year-old American marriage certificate and a notarized German translation of the same, but the really hard part was to produce 'positive proof' that we weren't divorced yet!

An especially happy aspect of this Sunday's gathering was that the relatives from East Berlin didn't have to show 'proof' that it was an important event just to go for coffee and cake to the old family home after twenty-eight years!

A Story about the Berlin 'Wallpeckers'

Berlin, December 1989

On December 2nd and 3rd, the young Canadian piano virtuoso Jon Kimura Parker gave two very successful concerts with the Berlin Radio Symphony Orchestra. Mutual Canadian friends alerted us to his coming and gave him our address. We agreed after his first concert to go on a short sightseeing tour the next morning. At 10 a.m. we had a 'smog warning' (one step below a smog alarm) with visibility next to nothing and a smell I don't care to describe. In spite of all this, Jon was sure that he wanted to go out to see the Wall.

Burk was literally 'under the weather', Charlotte had visitors from East Berlin, and Gabriella had a rehearsal for an afternoon concert with a chamber orchestra, so I took Jon to see the Brandenburg Gate and Checkpoint Charlie. As described before, the Brandenburg Gate is blocked by the thick 'dance wall' with a flat top. Most other sections of the wall around the city have a tube-like top, not suited for walking. Now a barricade keeps the tourists away from the 'dance wall', and two East German guards walk up and down on it, so the watchtower nearby is empty. In the below-freezing, smelly smog, this on-the-wall patrol is surely worse than sitting in a closed guard post.

After taking several pictures and buying two 'November 9' T-shirts, we walked towards the Reichstag, the former parliament building. There, the 'wallpeckers' were in full action. They are people who try to split off a piece of the wall by hammering away on it. The material is extremely hard, and most normal household hammers break before one gets even a little piece. The sound of a dozen hammers is like an orchestra of untuned triangles playing without a conductor. The great pianist looked at the scene longingly and said that he would very much like to have a piece of the Wall. Already well informed about the course of modern 'wall tourism', I pulled out a sturdy hammer and a heavy chisel from the canvas bag serving as my purse on this trip. This equipment belongs to our Leipzig tenant, whose parents worked in a large East German strip mining company. Jon was surprised and delighted. He wanted to go to work right away, but I insisted on wielding these bulky tools myself because I didn't have to play a piano concerto that evening. He gave in. Unfortunately, even my greatest efforts yielded only nickel-size pieces. Jon, for whom 'hammering' is part of his profession, hoped that he might be able to chip off bigger pieces. Concerto or not, he asked for the tools. I watched anxiously as he put the chisel at a right angle to the masonry.

His efforts attracted spectators. Two men trading critical remarks about his technique made comments like: "This man has never held a tool in his hands!" and "He surely couldn't earn a living with his hands; he is only fit to sit at a desk." I had to interrupt this talk and tell them that the target of their mockery had unusually skillful hands and that he earned his living as a concert pianist. Then they volunteered to show him how to chop the wall if they could hear him play the piano. We suggested that they might receive some tickets. One of the men took the equipment, swung the hammer high, and brought it down on the chisel with considerable force. A really big piece flew off. His second effort wasn't so successful. He hit his hand before he produced the second piece. Then we negotiated about the concert tickets for the evening, but it turned out that the two men with their wives were returning to Düsseldorf that afternoon. Jon said that he would probably play in the Düsseldorf Tonhalle next year and assured them tickets. The expert 'wallpeckers' wrote up their addresses and telephone numbers, and we parted in high spirits. Jon had a big piece of wall, and the man from Düsseldorf had an 'ouch' on his hand as a souvenir of this encounter.

At Checkpoint Charlie a Hungarian family lamented the loss of their wall-breaking tool. The son clutched the broken-off head of a normal household hammer. They rejoiced when I offered them my heavy East German equipment for a few minutes. My hands were hurting from too much wall-pecking anyway. In the meantime, Jon videofilmed the goings-on, but his collection was boosted with part of my yield from this site.

Gemology of the Wall: The inner city wall on the west side is completely covered with graffiti. The paint penetrates surprisingly deep into the stone. The outside of the wall is harder than the inside, so if one 'works' at a place where the surface has already been chipped off, then one gets bigger, but solid gray, pieces. Chopping away on the unbroken surface is very difficult, but the little pieces that one gets are very colorful.

Prospect for future tourists: The Wall has an almost unlimited bulk. Whenever a real hole arises, the East Germans fill it in overnight. Wall-pecking is officially forbidden, and at the Reichstag West Berlin policemen warn the people to stop. When the policemen walk on, the action continues. At Checkpoint Charlie large signs on the wall tell the tourists that hammering is forbidden. Still, lots of people do it. East German guards walk along the Western side and chase away the 'wallpeckers' every once in a while. One has to stop immediately, or they take away the tools. I just started hammering seconds after a guard had passed and finished when he approached on his return trip. They would probably react instantly if someone came with a power tool to get really big chunks. It is amazing how little the crowd excavates with the hand tools.

I close with a quotation from the East German political songwriter Wolf Biermann, who was not allowed to return to the GDR after East German authorities canceled his passport when he was on a tour of the West thirteen years ago. He then lived in the West, where he wrote critical songs about both East and West Germany. Upon his emotional return to Leipzig, he advised his countrymen in the refrain of his new song: 'Do not sell your country, just sell the Wall in little pieces as souvenirs!'

Epilogue

Post-wall Berlin is a chaotic city. The greatest change is the appearance of vast construction sites downtown, mostly on former Wall territory, where several buildings are sprouting simultaneously in a forest of tall cranes. The largest complex, a new 'city within the city', is emerging at Potsdamer Platz, a square with a varied history. With many streets and several subway lines crossing each other, it was a busy spot, like Piccadilly Circus in London, until World War II turned it into a heap of rubble. The Wall cut it into two, leaving the western part as a neglected field, where a large population of rabbits enjoyed the quiet no-man's-land status. Since the start of excavations for the foundations of the planned high-rises, the noise and the disappearance of the last bit of greenery have chased these animals away. Will they return when fresh green is planted near the new buildings?

There will hardly be any place for trees or bushes at the other extended construction site, the Checkpoint Charlie Business Center. Five huge buildings, each designed by a different American or German architect, will occupy the general area where the famous crossing point once stood. Although the checkpoint has ceased to exist, the name lives on not only in the newly erected Business Center, but also in the museum called 'House at Checkpoint Charlie'. This museum was established in 1963, a few meters from the control station and offered the first permanent exhibit about the Wall. Now it provides useful documentation on the twenty-eight dramatic years from 1961 to 1989.

The building activity makes its mark on the traffic in the form of detours and traffic jams. Travelers opting for public transportation do not escape the chaos either. The rapid transit system is also under construction and surprises abound. Trains do not stop at certain stations for several months at a time, and parts of subway routes are replaced by buses. Passengers who fail to consult the constantly updated bulletins can encounter incalculable delays.

Two topics related to the Wall are still widely discussed in Berlin. One concerns the lack of a feeling of unity among the population of East and West Berlin, and the other one is the question of how to treat the memory of the Wall.

An example of the first issue – that a 'Wall in people's minds' (*Mauer in den Köpfen*) still exists – was demonstrated by voting behavior in Berlin's municipal elections of October 1995. A color-coded map illustrating the results looks like an old East-West city map. Not one of the districts in the West has the same color as any in the East. The western districts were carried by the Christian Democrats and the Greens (Germany's environmental party); the eastern ones by the PDS (Party for Democratic Socialism – successor to the East German communist party) and the Social Democrats.

The second topic concerns arguments for and against documentation. People cannot agree whether the physical and historical aspects of the Wall should be kept alive. Those who favor documentation still disagree over the way in which it should be done, and groups that oppose it cite a variety of reasons for their standpoint. There is, for instance, an ongoing discussion about whether the former course of the Wall should be marked with a red line on the pavement throughout the city. Some Berliners are all for it, others are just not interested in spending money on such a project, whereas many are vehemently opposed to keeping track of the erstwhile dividing line.

In actual practice, the Wall was first almost completely dismantled and then rebuilt along certain prominent stretches. Given current construction plans and the price of prime real estate, these lengths of wall are bound to disappear again. Other sections might return to their original sites and find themselves incorporated into the hallways of large commercial structures. The only reliable place to see remnants that have not been moved is the East Side Gallery. This is a 1300 meter segment of the former hinterland wall on Mühlenstrasse in East Berlin. Artists were invited in 1990 to paint sections of this gallery, but their murals are not well protected from the weather, graffiti sprayers, and wallpeckers.

For the sake of interested tourists and of the next generation, I vote for continued documentation. With the passage of time, more and more people have been asking questions: where was the Wall? What was it like living with it? It is in this spirit that I have written these twenty-five short pieces. My wish is not to settle accounts with the bygone GDR regime, or to perpetuate the spirit of the cold war. Instead, my aim is to commit to paper encounters that were characteristic of the time and the system, but that are unlikely to find their way into history books.

The Wall influenced the lives of millions, among them the members of the extended family I married into. Our personal stories illustrate events and experiences that were shared by many other people. Although these occurrences were common in those days, by now they seem unreal.

It is extremely fortunate that the Wall 'dissolved' and disappeared without violence, thereby giving reason to hope that the same can happen to other unnatural barriers that still divide people.

Marianna S. Katona
Berlin, December 1996

To the Second Edition

Almost fourteen years have passed since the opening of the Wall and six since the first edition of this book. In this time great progress has been made in building up the capital city. Construction sites of a few years ago have transformed themselves into blocks of impressive buildings. Theaters, restaurants and offices alternate in the new downtown area around Potsdamer Platz. Glass dominates the architecture in this business and cultural center and also in the government district nearby. Even the heavy set Reichstag (Parliament) has been modernized with the addition of a glass dome. Considerable stretches of East Berlin have lost their earlier characteristic drab grayness. Restaurants, discos and small galleries have opened in attractively renovated apartment buildings not only in the center but also on the outskirts of the city.

Can one say that with the completion of new buildings and the renovation of old ones the unity of the city has been reestablished? Not quite. The attitude of the people has changed less than the outer look of the city. Each new election so far has shown that a large number of inhabitants feel collectively differently in the East than West. Nostalgia (*Nostalgie*) for the old East (*Ost*), fittingly called *Ostalgie,* is an attitude prevalent among some Easterners. Those stricken with it think (or know) that they were happier under the regulated and suppressive Communist system that took care of them – like strict parents of their children – while stifling their independence and creativity. Maybe fourteen years is not long enough for radical change, but a new generation of children is growing up into mixed east-west families, who will surely represent neither side, but establish a unified city and country.

Documentation of the historical past has also made progress. In the center of the city, such as along Stresemannstrasse (for this street with Wall, see photo section) and Zimmerstrasse the course of the Wall is marked by a double row of cobblestones set in the otherwise smoothly asphalted pavement. A brass line is visible on Niederkirchener Strasse when parked cars and tourist buses pull away from the curb in front of the Martin Gropiusbau (see page 80). An early form of the allied checkpoint booth was rebuilt on Friedrichstrasse in front of the Checkpoint Charlie Museum, replacing the later booth that was lifted away in 1990 (see page 83) and placed for posterity in the yard of the Allied Museum on Clay Allee. Dramatic Wall years are illustrated at the scene of events on Bernauer Strasse in a document center next to a reconstructed double-strand section of the Wall.

The interest of tourists young and old does not seem to wane with the passing of years. The memory of the Wall, the landmark that once upon a time cut through the now busiest middle section of this metropolis, is a gruesomely fascinating detail that still adds a special touch to the usual tourist fare offered by the cultural and scientific attractions of unified Berlin.

Marianna S. Katona
Berlin, July 2003